MWS Library

AMERICAN HERITAGE SERIES

AMERICAN HERITAGE SERIES (*Cont'd*)

Green Grows the Prairie

Green Grows the Prairie

(*Arkansas in the 1890's*)

by CHARLIE MAY SIMON

illustrated by Ernest Crichlow

ALADDIN BOOKS
New York: 1956

LIBRARY OF CONGRESS CATALOGUE CARD NUMBER: 56-5480

To the Three Park Sisters
Eva, Anne and Jane

CHAPTER I

◆ THERE WAS A SUDDEN HUSH among the men lounging on the porch of the post office when Jim rode up. Their talk had been loud and lively enough until then.

"Now if he had any get-up-and-get about him he'd go on out there, too, instead of —" Mr. Gilpin, the postmaster, had been saying. Then he stopped short as if he had been nudged to silence.

Jim knew they had been talking about him and about the letter waiting for him inside.

Little enough mail came to the Crossroads post office, and here was one from faraway

Seattle, Washington. The news of the arrival
of a letter had not been long in reaching the
farm where Jim lived with his sister Kitty and
her husband. And by the time he could
saddle the old mare, Trinket, and come to the
post office everybody else in the county knew
about the letter, too.

It could only be from Reuben. A year had
gone by since he'd boarded up the windows of
the farmhouse and sent Jim across the bayou
to live with Kitty. In the year there had come
only one letter—up to now.

"Oh, there are big things happening out
there in the world, I'm telling you," Reuben
used to say. "And I aim to find out what it's
all about."

To hear him talk, all a person had to do was
turn his feet from home, and he'd find a fortune waiting for him.

"A fellow can't get anywhere, here, on the
prairie," he had said to Jim when he left.
"I'm going to send for you as soon as I make
good, so you'll have your chance, too."

Reuben had only bought a railroad ticket
to Chicago but he had gone on to the West
Coast almost at once. His first letter had
come from Los Angeles. He had written,
then, that there was no future in California,

that he had heard great things about Seattle
in the State of Washington. He was leaving
for Seattle.

Months had passed and now there was a
letter waiting, postmarked Seattle. Reuben
must have liked it there. He must have made
good, Jim thought. Maybe the letter had a
railroad ticket inside. Maybe he was expecting Jim to join him out West right away.

The postmaster left the group of men on
the porch, and Jim followed him inside. He
made his way around barrels of flour and
sugar and pickles and crackers, to the counter
where the mail was kept. The soft drawl of
the men's voices drifted into the room as they
sat facing the open door.

"A hundred and five in the shade and no
shade. I've never seen the beat since the
summer of '74."

"Well, if a rain comes now, it'll be too late
for me, the way the corn's been drying up and
the cotton not even making."

"It's going to be a heap sight worse if that
man McKinley's elected President. We'll be
dragged into a war between Spain and Cuba
just as sure as you're born."

"And if he's not, we'll be dragged into the
poorhouse with that William Jennings Bryan

and his free silver," another voice answered
hotly.

Even as they spoke, they were watching Mr.
Gilpin as he looked through the little handful
of mail.

"Here it is," Mr. Gilpin said, and he read
aloud from the envelope before giving it to
Jim. "*Mr. James Luckett. July 28, 1896.*
That's just a week ago to the day, and I'd
call it making good time from the State of
Washington clear down to Arkansas."

Jim turned the envelope over in his hand,
hesitating to open it. A feeling of homesickness for the prairie came over him at the very
thought that he might be leaving.

"It's Reuben's handwriting all right," he
said.

"That's what I figured," Mr. Gilpin replied
and waited for Jim to open it and read it
aloud. Letters were not something you kept
to yourself; news from the outside world was
always shared.

Mrs. Gilpin came in from the living quar-
ters in the back of the store and took a seat
beside the window with her sewing in her lap.
Her needle went nimbly in and out of the
cloth but her eyes were fastened on the letter

in Jim's hand. When he tore it open, she stopped all pretense of working to listen.

Dear Folks: I hope this finds you all well, with Kitty and Jefferson happy in their marriage, and you, Jim, minding your manners and causing no trouble to your teacher and kin.

"Reuben always was one to give advice as if he were a bearded old man!" Jim said.

Since the death of their parents, Reuben had looked upon himself as head of the family. Of course he *was* the oldest—but even six years wasn't enough difference to make him act so fatherly.

"He's not sending for me yet," Jim said, reading quickly ahead. "He's been up in Alaska and that's why he didn't write before. He was at a place he calls Forty Mile, close to where the Klondike River empties into the Yukon."

"Well, what does he have to say about it?" one of the men called out from the porch as they all moved closer to the door.

Jim read in a voice loud enough for them all to hear:

There's been talk about a chance of finding gold there, but you can take my word for it, there's nothing to it. Anybody could tell that, from the way the willows lean and the creeks run wide and deep.

"Well, gold or not, I don't know but what I'd have stayed on if it had been me," Mr. Gilpin said. "I'd trade the heat of this summer any old time for a little of Alaska's snow and ice right now."

"As for me," another voice spoke up, "I'm giving this prairie one more chance. Just one more, mind you. If I don't do any better next year than I've done so far, I aim to go back where I came from. Back to God's country."

A short, heavy-set man had climbed out of his wagon and hitched his team to the rail. No one saw him coming until he started up the steps and spoke, in a quiet voice. "I'd say it's all God's country. Seems to me He made one place the same as He made another."

"Well, if it's not old Will Fuller," one of the men spoke up. "Thought for sure you'd gone back home to Illinois by now."

"My home's right here on the Arkansas prairie," Mr. Fuller answered.

"How are things around Hazen?" another

man asked. "Are the crops drying up there the way they're doing here? Half the county's given up and moved away."

Will Fuller stroked his small, pointed beard and thought a while before answering.

"Did you ever hear the story about the man down in South Africa who sold his farm so he could go off and search for diamonds?" he asked.

"And the fellow that bought it discovered diamonds right in his back yard. But what's that got to do with what we're talking about?"

"He means if we stick around, we'll find diamonds in our back yard. Wouldn't be surprised at that—the ground's baked hard as a seam of coal."

Will Fuller joined with the others in the laughter, but he had nothing more to say. He strode inside the store and looked over Mr. Gilpin's stock of guns. The talk turned to hunting and Jim's letter was forgotten.

Jim glanced quickly down to the end of the page; then he folded it and put it in his pocket. He bought a weekly newspaper, the *DeVall's Bluff Enterprise*, for his brother-in-law and a rattle with a pink ribbon bow for his little niece, Lucy. Then he got on his horse and started back home.

He was not sure whether to be glad or sorry
that he wouldn't be leaving Arkansas. At
midday, when he had started for Crossroads,
the prairie had been like an immense picture
some artist had started to paint, then put
aside, unfinished. There was a splash of dark
green on the horizon where a small grove of
trees grew beside the bayou. All the rest was
open sky and plain, colorless in the heat haze,
just dirt and dust and dry prairie grass.

Now, in late evening, when the sun was
low, the prairie had a beauty of its own. A
band of orange and red colored the western
sky and its glow was reflected everywhere. It
was a silent time of day. The meadow larks
and red-winged blackbirds had left off singing
and the chuck-will's-widows and screech owls
had not begun.

Even the prairie chickens and rabbits, hidden in the deep grass, were settling quietly in
their nests. There was no sound louder than
the sleepy hum of insects and the gentle breeze
blowing through the grass like a girl in long
skirts creeping stealthily.

"Get on, Trinket. It'll be dark as all get-
out before we get home as it is," Jim said,
patting his horse affectionately.

He spoke more to hear the sound of his own

voice than to hasten the horse's steps, for the
reins still hung loose in his hands. He made
no move to urge the mare on faster. The heat
lingered like a blanket and the blue clay earth
was like a hard stone beneath the horse's
hoofs. An animal as old as Trinket and worn
by years of work even before Reuben had
bought her must set her own pace on a long,
hot journey.

Jim's coat and vest were rolled up in a ball
on the saddle in front of him. As he rode on,
he loosened his stiff collar and untied his tie.
Then he reached down and took off his shoes
and socks and put his bare feet in the stirrups.

The houses that he passed were like polka
dots upon the prairie, set back as they were
from the road and scattered far apart. Many
were empty, abandoned by some discouraged
owner. And the fields, once plowed and
planted to cotton or corn, were grown over by
sedge grass.

His own home—the house they'd built
when they'd moved from Drew County—stood
empty like these others. But it wasn't deserted like these places—not yet anyhow.
Unless Reuben sent for him, Jim meant to
live in the house and farm the land, again, as
soon as he was grown.

A small, black object appeared on the horizon, another polka dot on the prairie, moving slowly along the road toward Jim. As it drew closer, he saw that it was a wagon, the back piled high with chairs and beds and tables. Another prairie farmer giving up!

Every year Jim saw people leave the prairie in defeat. But always before it had been after the harvest was over. Now, here was a family who wouldn't wait. They were leaving now, in mid-summer.

Jim pulled his horse to a stop when the wagon came alongside. He saw that they were neighbors who lived this side of his old homeplace. Mr. Hodges and his wife were on the seat in front, with one child between them and the other in Mrs. Hodges' lap. A cow was tied to the back of the wagon with her calf following close behind and a long-eared, spotted dog trotted underneath.

"I didn't know you planned to move, too," Jim said in surprise. "There wasn't any sign of it when I passed by your place on my way to Crossroads."

"I didn't know it myself till today," Silas Hodges said. "It came to me all of a sudden this morning when I looked out at my fields and saw nothing but dried-up corn stalks like

poles stuck in a row. Cotton growing so low to the ground a bumblebee would have to stretch its legs to reach the blossoms. I said to myself right then and there, 'I'm leaving this place. And I'm leaving it for good.' "

"Where are you figuring on going?"

"Back to God's country. Back to where we came from," the man answered. Then he added, "I take it you've been to Crossroads to get the letter that came for you."

"Yes. It's from Reuben."

"What's he got to say? Has he made good yet?"

Mrs. Hodges turned to Jim, too, and waited for his answer. If somebody had made good somewhere, that would be pleasant news.

"He's been up in Alaska," Jim said, "but he didn't get on well there. So he went on back to Seattle."

"Is that where he aims to settle? What did he say it was like?"

"He didn't say what it's like in Seattle. He's making plans to leave and go some other place."

"Well, I reckon a fellow wouldn't have to strike it rich to be a heap better off than he'd be if he stayed on in these parts. Don't know but what I'd go and join him anyhow, if I was in your shoes."

With these words, the man slapped the reins to urge his mule on.

"Good-by," Jim said. "And good luck."

"Good luck to you, son. You'll need it a heap worse than I will if you don't make up your mind to leave while the leaving's good. You follow Reuben—he had the sense to leave while he could."

There's something forlorn about seeing the backs of people turning away from their homes, Jim thought. It was strange how chairs and beds and bureaus could take on such an air of shabbiness, piled up in a wagon.

There was something forlorn, too, about land that was abandoned. Jim had heard old Indian fighters tell about certain tribes they had come across in the West who sent their old people off to die when the days of their usefulness were over. He could never look at empty houses and neglected fields after that without thinking of that tale.

"Back to God's country. Back where we came from."

The man's words came back to Jim. And he thought of Will Fuller saying in his slow, quiet voice as he came up the post office steps, "I'd say it's all God's country."

Drew County, where Jim was born, had been a pleasant place. It was six years since they had left it, but Jim could still remember the rolling hills and the path leading through the woods and the smell of pine on a summer day.

He'd walked a mile every day through the pine woods to school. The last year—that's when he was eight—his teacher had been Laura Morse. "Miss Laura" he'd called her and he could remember his mother laughing because the teacher wasn't more than fifteen years old herself.

Before school was out that summer, both Jim's parents were dead. Then the happy times in Drew County were over.

But the prairie had sounded like paradise, too, to hear Reuben talk when he first made up his mind they'd move here. He had read aloud to Jim and Kitty from the pamphlets the railroad company sent out, telling of this land they were putting up for sale.

We have beautiful rolling prairie land on each side of our tracks that would make the heart of an old Illinois prairie farmer dance with delight.

You didn't have to be an Illinois prairie farmer to listen with wide eyes to Reuben reading those pamphlets.

Three wild geese flew overhead on the way to their roosting place. They must have summered here, for it was too early for the fall migration and far too late for the spring. Had they stayed on of their own choice when their companions had flown north? And was it because they had not wanted to leave a place they'd grown to love?

The sun never shone on more fertile soil or more smiling landscapes of water, timber and varied scenery than you'll find in Prairie County, Arkansas.

In his mind Jim could hear Reuben's voice reading those pamphlets over and over.

Think of such a country! What a land this will be with our daily trains thundering through this splendid country. Fifty dollars per acre will be the value of these lands now selling for five. Fifty? Yes, one hundred and fifty dollars much of this land will command per acre.

Reuben hadn't been quite twenty-one, and a cousin had been made their legal guardian at the death of their parents. He was glad enough to be rid of any responsibility when

Reuben wanted to take over, as head of the family. He had signed the necessary papers to sell the small farm in Drew County and buy two hundred acres of prairie land.

"A hundred and fifty dollars for two hundred acres!" Reuben was always quoting figures in those days. "That's thirty thousand dollars our farm will be worth. Why, we'll all be as rich as lords!"

Jim had not been happy their first year in this treeless country. Neither had Kitty, his sister. But gradually they had grown to love it. Now, Jim felt that here was where he belonged, as much a part of the prairie as the meadow larks that nested in the tall sedge grass.

But Reuben had very soon begun to grow restless and talk about moving on. They were opening up the Cherokee Strip in Oklahoma where a man could go out and take his choice of land and claim it for his own. And there was Texas, where a man could make his fortune raising cattle.

Each year Reuben had talked up some new scheme for getting ahead in the world. But they had stayed on in the two-room house they'd built and had ploughed a few acres and planted corn and cotton. It was not until

Kitty married Jefferson Brooks who owned a farm across Two Prairies Bayou, that Reuben's chance came to leave.

Jefferson Brooks had come to claim the acres his father gave him. That was an interesting story, the way Jeff told it. Old Mr. Brooks and his wife decided that they would divide up all their property and give it to their children in their own lifetime.

"We have four children," Jeff's parents had said. "One for each season of the year. We'll go to live a part of the year with each child."

Then the father had cut four straws of different lengths and Jeff and his three sisters had drawn lots for the share of property that would be theirs. Jeff had drawn the largest piece—the prairie land.

As soon as his house was built and the first field ploughed he had come courting Kitty, wading across the bayou in the cool of the evening. Then, when the corn was almost ripe, they had married.

As soon as Jeff and Kitty were settled, not long after harvest time, Reuben had packed his bag.

"You can stay with Jefferson and Kitty long enough to get further on in your schooling," he'd said to Jim. "And just as soon as I make good, I'll send for you, and we'll go up in the world together."

The profits Reuben had once dreamed of making on the prairie were now forgotten. He wanted to sell the farm then and there. But with so many places abandoned and standing idle, no buyer could be found. And now in his letter he wrote more urgently of selling. Jim reached back in his trouser pocket and took out Reuben's letter. The light was dim but he could still make out the words.

If you haven't sold the farm by this time, you and Kitty get together and take whatever you are offered for it. It's a waste to keep it any longer, paying taxes and such, when there are big things going on away from there.

The rest of his letter had been about a new scheme for getting ahead—about the new horseless buggies men were experimenting with all over the country. Reuben was the kind who'd want to be right in among the first when something new was being tried out.

A horseless buggy? Jim tried to imagine what it would be like to see Jeff's buggy, or their own wagon come tearing down the road without a horse or mule to pull it. He laughed aloud at the very thought, and Trinket perked up her ears at the sound, and started to trot faster.

Jim thought of the postscript in the letter, and he grew serious again.

> You'd better sell Trinket, too. She's getting old and won't be worth anything much longer. Besides, there won't be any need for horses in a few years anyway.

"Don't you worry, little old Trinket." Jim had a way of talking to her as if she understood. "I'll not get rid of you if I can help it. Not even if you're the last horse left in all the world."

CHAPTER II

⬛ THEY CAME TO THE SIDE ROAD
that led to the old farm, and the horse made
a move as if to turn. There was a spring of
cool water near the house, and she liked
nothing better, on a day as hot as this, than
to stop and rest and take a long drink from it.
But Jim pulled at the reins to guide her
straight ahead.

"Not this time," he said gently. "We're
too late to make any stops now. You can get
a drink at the bayou. It will be almost as
cool as spring water, now that the sun's gone
down."

28

Twilight still lingered on the prairie, but the grove was like a dark room when Jim entered it. The trees were tall and close together, with leafy branches forming a ceiling over his head. Trinket slowed her pace, stepping cautiously into the shallow bayou. She stopped in midstream to drink.

Once on the other bank, Jim could see the light from his sister's window, appearing and reappearing through the trees like a star behind a moving cloud.

Tiger, Reuben's yellow dog, came out to meet Jim. He wagged his tail, but he didn't jump and frolic in a dog's dance of joy, the way he had done with his master. And when Jim had unsaddled the horse and fed her at the stall, Tiger trotted back to his bed under the house.

"That you, Jim?" Kitty called from the back door. She held the lamp high in her hand to light the way for him. "Come on. You must be half-starved. We've already eaten. It got so late we couldn't wait."

When she saw him with his shoes and socks in his hand, with his collar in his trousers pocket and the tie half hanging out, she began to scold.

"Jim Luckett, if you don't look a sight to

behold! I hope you didn't take off your clothes like that at Crossroads and disgrace us all in front of the people there."

Jim rumpled his sister's hair teasingly and followed her into the kitchen. He greeted Jeff and went over to the cradle where the baby

lay cooing and smiling up at him. He shook
the rattle he had brought her, and she waved
her little fists in the air, trying to grasp it.

"I vow, I believe Lucy knows you, Jim,"
Kitty said proudly.

"A good hound pup knows a person inside
of two months. Why shouldn't a baby be as
smart?" Jim answered.

"Oh, you!" Kitty exclaimed good-naturedly.
"Where's the letter? Was it from Reuben?"

"Yes," Jim replied, and his face grew serious
as he took it from his pocket.

Kitty glanced at the letter, then she handed
it to her husband.

"Here, honey. You read it out loud while
I press Jim's coat and vest. Tomorrow's Sunday and I don't want to have to do such work
then."

She put an ironing board across two
straight-back chairs, and with a padded cloth
she picked up an iron that she kept heating on
the back of the stove. Her hands moved
silently as she listened to Jeff read the letter.
Her bright eyes spoke for her, tender and
affectionate in the beginning for the absent
brother, then changing to a quick flash as Jeff
read on in his slow, soft drawl.

If you haven't sold the farm by this

time, you and Kitty get together and take
whatever you are offered for it.

"Well I can give my answer to that here
and now," Kitty spoke up before Jeff read any
further. "I'll do no such thing, and that's
that. What do you think, Jeff?"

Jeff was a gentle person and he weighed his
words well before he spoke.

"Well I'd say, since the farm belongs to all
three of you," he said at last, "and Reuben
wants to sell, but you don't, then it'd be up to
Jim here to decide what to do. He'd make
the majority, whichever side he'd choose."

"You men!" Kitty exclaimed impatiently.

"Well, Jim, what are you going to decide
then?" she asked.

"Don't hurry him," Jeff spoke up before
Jim had a chance to answer. "That's something a fellow has to think long and hard
about before he makes up his mind one way
or another."

He opened the paper Jim had brought home
and began to read the news aloud. The first
page had speeches by William Jennings Bryan
who was the Democratic candidate for the
Presidency and speeches by William Mc-
Kinley, the Republican candidate. Hot

speeches on both sides, for this was a bitterly fought campaign.

"Isn't there anything in the news except the presidential campaign?" Kitty asked. She was a woman and couldn't even vote if she wanted to. Politics seemed far away from her home on the prairie.

"You women!" Jeff laughed but obligingly turned the page.

"There's going to be an eclipse of the sun tomorrow," Jeff said. "A lot of folks have already gone off to Norway and Japan to see it better."

"Why can't they stay at home and see it?" Kitty asked. "Don't we have the same sun here as they do over there?"

"Yes, but we don't see it the same way at the same time," Jeff answered.

"Just the same, I'd like to see it too," Jim said.

They talked about everything but Reuben's letter though that was foremost in their minds.

Finally, as Kitty took the lamp into the front room to light the way to bed, she said impatiently, "I wish he'd take a notion to settle down. He can't go traipsing around forever."

CHAPTER III

JIM HAD A ROOM IN THE LOFT. His window was high up beneath the eaves where he could look out over the prairie as soon as he opened his eyes in the morning.

Somewhere out there toward the north, Reuben was traveling even now from West to East in search of something he could not explain. Jim tried to picture his brother but somehow the faces of those he scarcely knew were clearer to him than that of his own kin.

In his mind he could see old William Fuller again, with his steel-gray eyes and his funny little goatee beard. And he could see the men on the porch and neighbors in the houses he had passed. But it was only when he looked at his own reflection in the mirror that Reuben's face came back to him.

Everybody said Reuben and he looked just alike and Jim admitted they had the same deep-set, brown eyes and the same brown hair the color of oak leaves in the fall. They even had the same unruly lock of hair that fell down over the forehead in a cowlick, and would not stay brushed back.

But in their ways Jim knew that he and Reuben were as different as brothers could be. Reuben could never look out on a distant horizon without wanting to go and see what it was like beyond. But he missed the things close by; all the little things that made life exciting from day to day just passed Reuben by.

Like that prairie warbler, for instance, perched on a stalk in the cornfield, swaying to and fro like a child in a swing!

Its morning call was loud and clear, rising up and up in the scale. And from the grove beyond, a woodthrush joined in with a sweet, flute-like song that seemed to have no beginning and no end. And there was a young doe grazing near the field, as unafraid as any

animal in the barnyard. As Jim watched, the
sun rose and then the doe went bounding
away, to disappear in the willow thicket close
to the bayou.

From the high window, the island of trees
seemed closer than from the ground. Something dark and shadowy was moving stealthily
through the underbrush. It might be the
deer, or it might be a wolf or bobcat, or even
a black bear.

Beyond the grove, across the bayou, was
their own place—the farm Reuben wanted to
sell, and Kitty wanted to keep. The choice
of whether they sold or not was Jim's to make.
Suppose they did take whatever they could
get? Prairie land was worth no more than
fifty cents an acre, now, instead of the hundred and fifty dollars the railroad company
had predicted. And the house, vacant now
as so many were, wouldn't bring much. But
whatever amount they did receive, there would
be enough for him to buy a railroad ticket and
go away as Reuben had done.

"I could go anywhere I want," Jim thought.
"I could decide for myself where it would be,
just like Reuben and all the others."

He could get on the train at DeVall's Bluff
and go to Memphis. And from there he could

go north, south, east or west and make his way in the world.

But no matter where he went, the prairie would always call him back. Looking out over the wide expanse of sky and earth with its polka dot islands of green trees, gave him a sense of freedom. How would it feel to have mountains or forests or city buildings closed in around him?

Besides, there was Trinket. She was not like Tiger, loyal only to the absent Reuben. Trinket had come to look upon Jim as her master, and even now she must be waiting beside the barnyard gate for him to come and feed her.

Jim poured water from the china pitcher into the bowl on the washstand to wash his face and hands before putting on his clothes. He could hear Kitty and Jefferson moving about downstairs. It was Sunday, but on a farm there could be no late rising for there were always chores that must be done.

Kitty was singing a song about broken hearts when Jim came downstairs. But her voice was gay.

After the ball was over. After the break of day. She rolled a batch of dough on a floured board and cut out biscuits in rhythm to her

song. *Many the hearts that were broken—*
Jim could scarcely remember his mother
when she was well and active, for she had
been an invalid from the time he was a baby.
It had been up to Kitty to do the work about
the house since she was barely old enough to
hold a broom or wash a dish. Even now, with
a home and family of her own, there was
something about her half-playful, half-serious
air that reminded Jim of a little girl putting
on long skirts and pinning up her hair to play
lady.

"Jim, honey" (she called everyone in the
family *honey*), "when you go out to feed the
chickens I wish you'd catch a couple of fryers.
Put them in a coop, just in case company
comes today. But make sure you don't catch
Biddy, that little white leghorn."

There was always some special pet Kitty
claimed among the chickens or pigs and ducks
and geese which she could not bear to kill
or sell.

"There are at least a dozen little white
leghorn hens out there. How am I going to
know which one is Biddy?" Jim asked, helping
himself to a crisp fried bacon rind from a
platter on the back of the stove.

"Oh, you'll know her all right. She's the

one that will come and eat right out of your hand if you let her. And keep away from those cracklings. I won't have a one left for the cornbread the way you and Jeff have been picking at them."

Kitty tried to frown, but her dark eyes sparkled merrily in spite of herself. "Make haste now. And tell Jeff to hurry, too, for we'll want to make an early start if we're going to get to church on time."

Her last remark was needless, for Sunday chores were always done and over with as quickly as possible. Tiger stirred from his bed under the house and came out to greet Jim with an uncertain wag of his tail. Then, as always, he turned and went away, refusing to follow.

But Timmie, the white cat, came walking through the fields from the direction of the bayou and met Jim on his way to the barn. She rubbed her back against his leg and purred, and Jim leaned down to stroke her.

"Where do you go every night anyway? Wherever it is, you must like it there. You only show up here at meal time."

The cat scampered playfully along with him, running ahead a little way, then lying down in the path until he caught up. She'd bounce up then, and run a little farther, until they reached the barn where Jeff was milking the cow.

"The cat's a little late this morning," Jeff said with his slow smile. "She's usually here waiting beside her saucer for me when I come out to milk."

Jeff was about Reuben's age, but his serious expression and his moustache made him seem much older. He and Jim did their chores together as two brothers might.

"I'm not much on talking, Jim, but there's something on my mind I'd like to say," Jeff began in his slow, deliberate way. "I've no brother of my own, but if I had, I'd feel no different toward him than the way I feel toward you. And I want you to look upon this place as your home, too, the same as if we were blood kin."

It was a long speech for Jeff to make, and Jim knew that he was trying to tell him there was no need for him to feel he had to go away as Reuben had advised.

"I'm much obliged, Jeff," Jim answered. "I guess I've felt it all along without your telling me."

Jeff stooped to pour some milk in the cat's saucer. Then, as if ashamed of having shown his feelings too much, he picked up the milk pail and started back to the house without saying another word.

Jim shelled some corn and scattered it to the chickens. The little leghorn, Biddy, came running up to take it from his outstretched hand. It would have been easy enough to catch her. But the others were as wary as wild prairie chickens and darted off beyond his grasp if he so much as made a move. He cornered two at last, and put them in a pen.

Then he went on to feed the horses. He left Jeff's horse in the stall and turned Trinket out to pasture.

"No, Trinket," he said when the mare lingered at the gate and would not go off to graze. "You'll have to stay at home today and let Beck take us to church. You had enough exercise yesterday, going to Crossroads in all that heat. I'd think you'd be glad enough of a rest today."

The mare nudged her nose playfully against the palm of his hand. Sometimes he wondered if she couldn't really understand him when he talked to her. Good old Trinket. She wasn't much to look at, bony as she was with all her ribs showing no matter how much he fed her, and so swaybacked she must have been born that way. She wouldn't win a prize at a horse show. And in a race she'd be likely to come in last.

"But I won't get rid of you," he said as he patted her neck. "I'll think of some way I can keep you."

He walked back to the house, going over in his mind a dream he had had the night before. He had dreamt that he had found silver dollars scattered over the ground. As fast as he could pick up one dollar, he'd see another, and then a little distance beyond there'd be still another until his pockets were full and sagging with the weight.

He told the dream as he sat down at the breakfast table. "If I tell it before breakfast, it might come true," he said in a joke.

But Kitty listened seriously. She took up a platter of fried ham and eggs and stood holding it in her hand, forgetting to put it down.

"It's a sign, Jim," she said when he had finished telling it. "It means you ought to stay right here where you'd be better off than if you went away from home as Reuben did. Don't you think so, honey?" she went on, turning to her husband.

"Maybe so," Jeff answered, and though he did not smile, his eyes had a teasing expression.

"And again maybe he had his mind on what
we've been reading in the paper he brought
home last night, about William Jennings
Bryan and his talk about free silver."

"Oh you!" Kitty exclaimed. "I don't know
what they mean by free silver. It's not free,
is it?"

She took a pan of biscuits out of the oven;
then she piled three plates high with batter-
cakes swimming in melted butter and ribbon-
cane molasses.

"I remember a time when I was a little
girl back in Drew County. I wasn't more
than three years old, and you, Jim, were not
even born," she said. "The sun had come out
right after a rain, and Reuben saw the rain-
bow. He set out then and there, thinking
he'd walk to the end of it where he would
find a pot of gold. I went tagging along, as
usual, but I couldn't keep up with him for he
walked too fast for me. I had to turn around
and go back home.

"When I came within sight of our house,
the sun was just going down, and I could see
our windows blazing in the light like they'd
been turned to pure gold. I ran as fast as
I could, pleased and at the same time mad

as I could be at Reuben. There he was, walking to the end of the world when we had golden windows right at home."

"Well, we're not going to find either silver dollars or golden windows here," Jeff said. "All we're likely to find is hard work and plenty of it. But it's home, and that's enough."

"Yes," Kitty agreed. "It's home, and that's enough." Then she turned to Jim and asked, "Have you made up your mind yet about whether you want us to sell the farm or not?"

"My mind's been made up all along about that. I don't want to sell it any more than you do. But there's one thing I can't help thinking of. It's what Reuben had to say about selling Trinket, too. She belongs to Reuben and he has full say about what to do with her. He might be needing the money she would bring. I have to think of some way to buy her and keep her here."

"Something will turn up," Kitty said cheerfully. "Come on. We'd better hurry if we don't want to be late for church."

Jim nodded and went to get the shoe blacking to polish his shoes, but Jeff did not stir.

"Maybe if our cotton does well this year we

could buy out Reuben's share of the land," he said. "If money's needed for his new venture that would only be fair."

Cotton—Jim shined his shoes until he could almost see his own reflection in them, as if he could brush away the problem with the dust. He knew that cotton was not the answer to raising the money and he guessed that Jeff knew it too.

Without more words Kitty's menfolk got into their blue Sunday suits and white shirts with collars starched so stiff they could scarcely turn their heads.

Jeff looks as uncomfortable as I feel, Jim thought gloomily.

But Kitty loved dressing up, no matter how hot the weather. Her small waist was laced tight to make it still smaller, and the leg-of-mutton sleeves on her dress were starched so that they stood out like white wings from her shoulders. She had dressed Lucy in a long, white dress.

"You remember this, don't you, Jim?" Kitty asked, showing him the dress with its rows of lace and tucks and ruffles.

It was his own christening dress and it had been kept all the years until Lucy was born in tissue paper in a trunk.

"I remember seeing it, but I don't remember wearing it," Jim answered with a laugh.

"Who'd ever think, to see you now standing there bigger than I am myself, that you were ever as little and sweet as Lucy here," Kitty said.

Jim held out his hand to Lucy and she grasped his finger firmly, and gave him an understanding, toothless grin. He looked down at his own large hand and compared it with hers.

"Wouldn't it be funny if we kept on growing all our lives as much as we do from the time we're born till we are fourteen."

"By the time we were ninety we'd be taller than the biggest cypress on the bayou," Kitty said. "We could step across White River in just one step or two, and it wouldn't take us more than fifteen minutes to walk to town."

"I'd never be able to ride Trinket unless she grew too. And houses and barns would have to be built big enough to hold us all," Jim went on with the game of suppose, just as he and Kitty used to do when they were small.

Jeff had hitched his horse, Beck, to the buggy. "Are you ready?" he called, from the gate.

"Law! Let me take one last look around

first," Kitty said, glancing about the front
room which served as bedroom and parlor.
"We'll have company coming back with us as
sure as you're living. It happens every time
I catlick this way in cleaning house. And
those two forks I dropped!"

Kitty longed for the kind of parlor she had
seen in the stylish houses of town and she
often talked of having another room added
after their first good crop was in. Until then,
she must make the front room as much like a
parlor as she could, with the tall walnut bed
and washstand set in a corner of the room.
The horsehair sofa and chairs were placed
near the hearth and a round parlor table
stood nearby with a plush photograph album
and the family Bible on it.

The sun beat down mercilessly on them as
they rode toward the church in the buggy.
The same small one-room building, standing
alone on a flat bare field between two prairie
farms, served as church on Sundays and school
on weekdays in the winter.

Even inside the church house the heat
lingered on, and palm leaf fans were waving
right and left noiselessly. Jim sat on the
bench that was his place in the classroom too.
Weekdays, he spelled aloud from a bluebook

speller. Or studied in his history book about people who lived long ago, when Columbus crossed an unknown ocean or when Caesar led his mighty armies. Sundays, he sang hymns and listened to the preacher and counted flies lighting on the window sill.

Jim looked at the people on the benches around him, dressed in their Sunday clothes, resting this one day out of seven from their week of work. Were there people such as these, going about their own affairs quietly while Columbus sailed away and Caesar's armies fought? And would the things happening now be written down in history books for children not yet born, to study? The Cuban Revolution? The presidential campaign now going on in this country? Was that history, too?

When the congregation rose to sing, Lucy began to coo and Kitty put her finger to her lips to hush her. The droning voice of the preacher reading his text from the Bible took Jim's thoughts back to a time still further in the past.

"And David put his hand in his bag and took hence a stone, and slang it, and smote the Philistine in the forehead—"

Jim thought of the young boy of ancient

Israel, who must have been about his own age, conquering the giant Goliath and saving his people from the enemy. He felt a closeness then for this boy, and for all people everywhere and through all the ages.

The congregation was smaller than it used to be. Many of the benches were empty, as they were on schooldays, too. That was because of the farms being abandoned, with more people moving away every season.

When the services were over, the people stopped outside the church to visit a little while before going on their way home.

"Come spend the day with me." The words were spoken over and over again.

And the answer always was, "We'd best be getting on, thanks. But you come home with us."

"I dropped those two forks this morning when I was setting the table for breakfast," Kitty said as they rode back home alone. "I thought for sure there'd be two people visiting with us for the day. I guess it's just too hot to go a-visiting."

"It wouldn't surprise me to find Ma and Pa waiting for us when we get back," Jeff spoke up.

"Well, it's about time your parents came," Kitty answered. "Your sister Nellie's had them long enough. It's not right for her to go on keeping them."

"With three daughters and a son, we've a child for each season of the year," old Mr. Brooks had said when they gave their property to their children.

The friends of the old couple had warned them against dividing up their property while they were still alive. "You'll end in the poorhouse as sure as they were born if you give away everything you own," the friends had predicted. "You know what happened to that king in Shakespeare's play . . . King Lear—"

"You don't know our children if that's what you think," both Mr. and Mrs. Brooks had answered.

And the welcome that met them whenever they arrived proved the old couple right.

"Just think, they've never seen Lucy, their own grandchild," Kitty said. "I think it's a shame."

But there was no horse and buggy in the yard, no one waiting on the front steps. Since no company had come, the chickens caught that morning were kept in the coop for another time, and Kitty cooked a quick snack of spoon bread and salad greens. It was too hot to eat much anyway, Kitty said.

They sat on the porch after the meal was over, but it was no cooler there than on the inside. A few spindly trees grew close by, too small to give much shade. Jeff had dug them up and brought them in from the grove. But they were little taller than on the day they had been transplanted. Their leaves scarcely stirred in the still air, and not a bird could be heard even from the grove.

"We could use that eclipse they're havin' in Norway," Jim said. "I wouldn't mind if the sun went behind the moon's shadow and stayed there for a while."

He had taken off his Sunday clothes and put on his comfortable, everyday ones.

"It gives a fellow a funny feeling, though, to see an eclipse," Jeff answered. "Even the animals know something strange is happening when dark comes while the sun is still high in the sky. Horses act skittish and try to run away. Cows go off to their stalls and low the way they do when they've lost a calf.

"The chickens go to roost, too, but they don't have sense enough to stay scared like any other animal. They come right out again as soon as it's over, and scratch and peck in the dirt. But you couldn't get a cow out of the stall to save your life till the next day.

"An eclipse is a pretty sight, I've been told," Kitty said. "The sun's hidden except there's a ring of fire all around it with colors like you'd never see at any other time."

"Does it turn cooler when the sun's hidden?" Jim asked.

"Yes. It makes no difference how hot the day's been, you feel chilly all of a sudden."

"I know one way to get cool," Jim said, and went down to the bayou for a swim.

The water was warm and sluggish, and he paddled lazily in it. Then he turned on his back to float, looking up at the leafy branches and the patches of blue sky that showed through.

Little shinners and towbellies that swam near the surface went scurrying out of the way as he drew near. Now and then a pin oak acorn fell with a splash in the water. Everything was so quiet that the sound was like an explosion.

When he had had enough of swimming, Jim stretched out on a bed of leafmold in the grove. There was no sign of any other living creature near. He might have been alone in a world that stood still.

In the mud along the water's edge, he could see footprints like those of some small baby that had been romping and playing. There were the marks of five little toes and a heel the size and shape of Lucy's foot. "Raccoon tracks," Jim said to himself. "Old 'coon must have come here last night to fish for its supper."

Wild lobelias and monkey flowers bloomed in blue and purple clusters, with the flame-like spike of the cardinal flower growing among them.

Gradually, as Jim lay there, too comfortable and lazy to move, the grove came back to life. A stir among the monkey flowers showed a squirrel, sitting as still as a piece of wood, with its tail curled over its head. Jim realized the animal had been there all the while, watching him with little shoebutton eyes. Leaves began to rustle and bushes swayed, and soon there were sounds of birds and insects and animals warbling, chirping and cooing softly.

A white heron flew clumsily to perch on the dead, bare branch of a sycamore. And a turtle, so still it might have been a fallen log, dived suddenly into the water. Jim closed his eyes drowsily. From a distance he could hear Tiger barking, and Trinket and Jeff's horse neighing. It was as if these sounds were part of a dream and not real at all. The sun shone slanting through the leaves upon his face, and he reached for his hat to put over his eyes.

It seemed to Jim that he had barely drifted off to sleep when he awoke to a twilight darkness. Tiger was still barking and the horses still neighing. Now he heard the cow begin to low.

He sat up suddenly. Could this be the eclipse? And had it happened here in Arkansas instead of in Norway and Japan as the learned men had expected?

A raccoon that was sideling down the trunk of a pecan tree turned its funny, clown-like face to stare at him. Then it scurried quickly to a high branch where it was hidden from view. The squirrel was gone, and the heron had flown away.

The cardinals and thrushes were silent, and there were sounds of night birds instead. Cicadas and katydids kept up a loud chorus from the prairie fields, and frogs in the bayou joined in with their croaking.

Jim hurriedly put on his clothes and went

out of the grove to the open plain. He searched the sky, but instead of seeing a darkened sun with a ring of fire around it, he saw instead, the thin sliver of a new moon. There was a bright star near it, and as he gazed, he saw another and another.

Then, all of a sudden, the sky was full of stars; the Big and Little Dipper, the North Star, and the bright Milky Way. He had slept the afternoon away, and this was no eclipse at all.

He heard Jeff's voice calling and he answered.

"Jim Luckett! Where on earth have you been? We've been calling our heads off for you," Kitty said when he came near.

"I've been asleep down at the bayou, and I'm as hungry as a bear in springtime."

"Well come on and wash up," Kitty said as she held up the lamp to light the way. "We're just getting ready for supper ourselves, for company's come after all. I knew dropping those two forks was a sign."

CHAPTER IV

SEATED AT THE SUPPER TABLE was William Fuller, the farmer from Hazen, with a tall, lanky man whom Mr. Fuller called Hewett Puryear. They'd been riding by, Jeff explained, in a covered wagon, going all the way to Louisiana to hunt in the swamps close to the gulf.

"It was mighty near dark when I saw 'em passing," he drawled, "so of course I persuaded them to stop and pass the night. We don't get people passing so often that we can afford to let 'em get away!"

Mr. Fuller recognized Jim when he came

into the room, and spoke to him as one man to another. But the stranger had a teasing manner and treated Jim as if he were a child.

"Look here, boy, wouldn't it be mighty risky to go to sleep out yonder in the woods with night coming on. It's just pure luck some varmint didn't tear you to pieces before you knew what was happening.

"German fellow I once knew, was passing through these parts. He went to sleep out in the woods by himself, just like you did today, young fellow," Mr. Puryear said. "When he woke up he found that he'd been covered up with dead leaves.

"He knew right away what that meant. A panther had been there, and she'd buried him and gone back to her den to get her young so they could all eat him together.

"Well, that German got up so fast you'd think he was a streak of lightning, so scared every hair stood on end. He heard a sound coming through the underbrush, and he ran to a tree a little way off and climbed up in it to hide. Sure enough, there came the old she-panther and two spotted little ones frolicking beside her. Lucky for him he had his gun along, or there'd have been nothing left of him to tell the tale."

"You hear that, Jim," Kitty said anxiously.

She took the baby up in her arms and crooned a gentle lullaby, as if she had no more interest in the talk of the men but her eyes sparkled as she listened. There were tales told of panthers in the old days that waited, crouched in the fork of a tree, ready to pounce on anyone passing that way. Many an old-timer had had a horse balk and refuse to go farther on a dark and lonesome trail because he knew, somehow, that danger lay ahead.

Through their talk, Kitty's voice could be heard crooning softly.

Hush little baby, don't say a word.

Papa's going to buy you a mockingbird.

"There wouldn't be any panthers this near a farm though," Jim said. "I hear them scream sometimes at night, but it's always far away, off in the direction where nobody lives."

"Animals leave when men come in," Mr. Fuller said. "There'll come a time when there won't be any animals left on the prairie except rabbits and field mice."

"Or else not any men, seeing how folks are leaving," Hewitt Puryear grunted.

Jeff told how his father had seen buffalo and elk in the early days in Arkansas, but the last of them had disappeared long ago. And they could all remember the time when passenger pigeons came flying through, darkening the sky with their numbers.

Sometimes there'd be so many roosting on the trees at night that the branches broke with their weight. And all a hunter needed to bring them down was a heavy stick. But there were none passing that way now. Even the prairie chickens were fast disappearing.

"They'll all be coming back and taking over again pretty soon, the way folks are leaving the prairie these days," Hewitt Puryear insisted.

An expression of annoyance came over Mr. Fuller's face at the man's words. Jim had noticed the same expression at the Crossroads post office the day before at any mention of how the prairie was being abandoned.

"How's hunting here at Two Prairies Bayou?" Mr. Fuller asked Jeff, as if to change the subject.

Kitty, who had stopped her song, took it up again.

If that mockingbird won't sing.
Papa's going to buy you a finger ring.

"It's fair to middling, hunting in these

parts," Jeff answered. "A few deer and now and then a bear in the island grove. But mostly squirrels and rabbits in the fields."

"And lean and bony at that, I'd say," Mr. Puryear went on. "There's mighty little around here for an animal to feed on. Not even a young boy that'd be plump enough for a square meal."

He looked at Jim, with his long legs doubled under the rung of his chair. Then he turned to the other men with a wink.

"Hewitt says there's good hunting down in Louisiana close to the Gulf," Mr. Fuller said, paying no attention to the man's joke. "That's the reason we're on our way there."

Puryear nodded. "I know because I've been there before. Bears are as thick as flies in those swamps. They're so fat they can scarce waddle this time of year, on all that corn and sugar cane they steal."

The two men shared Jim's room in the loft that night. He let them sleep in his bed and he made a pallet for himself on the floor. Mr. Fuller stood looking out the window after the lamp was blown out, like a shadow in the dark room. Jim could see only the outline of his short, squat figure with his little goatee beard and his voice came low and quiet through the darkness.

"It takes me back to the time I lived in Nebraska, seeing the prairie like this from a loft window in the dark of the moon," he said. "Only there, I'd see wheat instead of cotton in the field next to the corn."

"And growing a heap sight better than any crop here, I'd say," Mr. Puryear mumbled from his pillow.

"Yes. Wheat is a kind of grass, and grass will always grow well on a prairie," Mr. Fuller replied.

"Would it grow here?" Jim asked, raising up on his pallet with sudden interest. Maybe wheat was the crop to grow on the land across the bayou. Maybe a wheat crop could save the farm and pay Reuben his share.

"I could answer that one," Mr. Puryear spoke up. "No, it won't. It's been tried time and again by every Northern prairie farmer that's ever come here. Every crop has been a failure, like all the other things we've tried to plant."

"Wheat needs cooler nights than the ones we have down here in Arkansas," Mr. Fuller said quietly.

Jim sighed. Then growing wheat was not the answer. They'd have to depend on Jeff's cotton again. Well, anyway, he was glad he'd decided to stay here on the prairie. He thought of the old homeplace, empty now and getting shabby from not being lived in.

"I'll wade across the bayou and look it over tomorrow," he thought as he closed his eyes sleepily. "I'll think of a way somehow, to keep it till I'm old enough to live there and work it myself."

CHAPTER V

☞ THE HEAT AND DROUTH LINGERED on through August. The sun rose in a cloudless sky and went down in the evening in a dusty, yellow glow. Dust covered every tree and every blade of grass, and it rose in swirling thick clouds from wagons and buggies passing along the prairie road.

The water in the bayou was low and trickled sluggishly, choked with leaves that had fallen too soon. There were no birdsongs in the grove except the shrill cry of a woodpecker or a jay bird scolding harshly.

Farmers looked up to the sky for signs of

rain. Was the morning sky red? Would the rain crow give its call? They looked to see if the sun or the moon was pale, for that, too, might mean a change of weather. But all this was from force of habit for it was too late now for rain to do any good.

"The cow's been lowing all day, and I never knew the chickens to be so noisy," Jeff said one hot evening. "Maybe that means it's going to rain."

"And have you noticed how the lampwick sparks and sputters?" Kitty replied.

Jim nodded. "And the wild bees have been flying in a straight line, quickly to their hives in the island grove," he said. "Beside that— listen to the frogs croaking down by the bayou."

But there were as many signs of hot, dry weather as there were of rain. A white mist rose every morning before the sun came out, and bats flew early in the evening before it went down. The stars blazed red as if they were sparks of fire rising from a chimney. Now and then one could be seen shooting across the sky, leaving a trail of fire behind it.

Some said a shooting star was a soul going to heaven and others said somebody had done a good deed and the star was taking its place in his crown. But whatever it meant, the prairie farmers looked to see the direction it was falling from, for the rain clouds would surely come from there, they said.

As the month moved on, other visitors came to Jeff's and Kitty's house. Some spent the night and some stayed for the noon meal. But more stopped no more than an hour or so and then went on their way.

These were the agents who went from farm to farm showing their wares. They brought catalogues and pamphlets that told of everything from sewing machines and stoves to fruit trees and enlarged crayon portraits. This was the time they came to take orders. In the fall when the crops were harvested, they would return to deliver their goods and collect the money.

Kitty looked longingly at an enlarged crayon portrait of a child wearing a blue dress and holding a bouquet of flowers in her hand. The baby in the picture was about Lucy's age, with hair as yellow and eyes as large and brown.

"It was made from a little photograph," the agent said. "Now, all you have to do is give me a picture you want enlarged. I'll bring you back a handsome portrait like this, all framed and ready to hang on your wall.

It's the latest style, and there's scarcely a home in the country without one."

"It would be pretty to have one of Lucy hanging up there over the mantel," Kitty said. Then she added with a sigh, "Maybe we can next time you come this way, when our cotton's picked and sold."

She let the agent go without giving him an order. It was the same with Jeff when the fruit tree agent came that way. He studied the catalogues and named the fruit trees he'd like to plant. There were pictures of apples and peaches and pears looking so real that it made a person's mouth water just to see them on the page.

"An orchard might do well here, but it's something I'll have to wait and think over first," he said as he gave the catalogue back to the agent.

The book agent was the one who held Jim's interest most. There were sample books with only enough printed pages to make a person want to read on and see what was coming next. The rest of the pages were blank. But all the illustrations were there, and they gave a tempting hint as to what the rest of each book was about.

There were books that told of faraway

places and books of things that happened long
ago. And there was a book with speeches by
famous orators. On Friday afternoons, at
school, everybody spoke pieces they had
learned by heart. With a book such as this
you'd have no trouble choosing a knockout
speech. But Jim said "no" as Kitty and Jeff
had done.

There was no way of telling whether there
would be anything left after the harvest to
spend on such things as books and enlarged
crayon portraits. They'd have to wait and
see.

"Yes, I understand," the book agent said
with a nod of his head. "I haven't made a
single sale on the prairie. Close to the river,
it's different. The cotton, there, is shoulder
high and there's just as good a stand of corn."

Jim followed the man to the gate and stood
there watching him put the book dummies and
catalogues in the saddlebags and mount his
horse to ride away. The horse was a chestnut
mare, with silky hair and clear, bright eyes.
She held her head high and lifted her feet with
a lively snap as if she were eager to be off.

"You've got a fine horse there," Jim said
admiringly.

"Yes. We earn our living together, this

horse and I," the man answered with a proud smile. "I couldn't do my work without her, and it's a sure thing she couldn't get along without me."

When the agent rode on his way, Jim turned and looked toward the pasture where Trinket grazed. Bony and swayback, she couldn't be compared to the fine chestnut now trotting down the road and out of sight.

"Trinket's as ugly a horse as any I've ever seen," Jim said to himself. "But she's smart. She's got as much sense as any chestnut mare, and she'd be just as good at helping a fellow earn a living too."

Jim tried to think of some way he and Trinket could earn money together. But even if he thought of something he knew he couldn't start out until the crops were picked and the harvest in. And on the prairie, if anything brew at all, it matured late.

Harvest time did not come until the end of September. On the same day they started getting in the corn, Jeff's parents arrived.

Jim looked up from the cornfield and saw a rickety, old buggy drawn by a spirited, dapple-gray horse trotting down the road in a swirl of dust. "It's your folks," he called to Jeff. Kitty came running out of the house at the same time. She had seen them from the window.

"Well it's about time," Kitty scolded affectionately. "We were beginning to wonder if you'd ever get here."

Mrs. Brooks' hands were folded primly on her lap, and she wore a white lace collar over a black alpaca dress. Her gray hair was parted in the middle and drawn tightly back in a knot, and on the top of her head was perched a little, be-ribboned, black bonnet. But her keen eyes darted and sparkled, missing nothing.

Old Mr. Brooks wore a beard, as he had when he was a young Confederate soldier over thirty years ago. Now it was white instead of brown.

His wife waited until he stepped out first and held out his hand to help her. "Miss Lucy" he still called her, and he was always "Mr. Brooks" to her.

Jeff took in the big carpetbag and a smaller one that folded out like an accordion. The old couple walked up the path like some tintype picture come to life.

Jim drove their buggy to the shed, fed the horse and then turned him out to pasture with Trinket and Beck. When he returned to the

house, the two women were chattering like
magpies together, while Jeff and his father sat
smoking their pipes in silence. Mrs. Brooks
held Lucy, her namesake, in her lap. She
talked first to the child and then to Kitty until
her conversation was so mixed up it was hard
to follow.

"My, my, what a big girl you are. And
bright as a button, too," she said. "And what
do you hear from Reuben?"

"He's gone to Chicago or somewhere
around there, to learn about how horseless
carriages are made," Kitty answered.

"Law me, the world moves so fast it's all a
body can do to keep up with it," Mrs. Brooks
went on. "Carriages running without horses!
Think of that now! Next thing, they'll think
of some way we can tie wings on our arms and
go flapping around over the sky like birds, or
like angels. We can see for ourselves what
goes on up yonder then."

"That time the stars fell," Mr. Brooks broke
in suddenly. He had a way of talking about
something that happened long ago as if it were
only yesterday. "The Yankees took Little
Rock and we were in retreat. The stars fell
that night, shooting like rockets through the
sky, and thick as lightning bugs in a cane

brake. We thought for sure the world was coming to an end. And when the bugle blew for reveille, we near about jumped out of our skins, thinking it was the angel Gabriel blowing his horn."

He had told the story many times, but everybody laughed with him as if they had never heard it before.

After supper that night, Jim gathered up a roll of bedding, a lantern and a bucket and dipper. It had been planned ahead of time that he would sleep nights at the homeplace across the bayou, during the old couple's visit. However, they protested when they saw him leave.

"We're not going to put you out," Mrs. Brooks said. "We can sleep as well on pallets as on a feather bed, for we've done it many a time before."

"Now, Mamma Brooks, you might as well stop talking that way, for you're going to have our bed down here, and Jeff and I will take the baby and go up to Jim's room in the loft. After all, it's not your fault we haven't got around to adding that extra room," Kitty said.

Mrs. Brooks smiled and patted Kitty's cheek. "Folks used to say to me, having three daughters and one son, 'A daughter's a daughter all her life, but a son's a son till he gets him a wife.' But now I tell them it's not so. I've got my son and I've got another daughter as well."

Jim was glad enough to have a reason for going back to the old place. It would be like camping and, at the same time, it would be like returning home after a long voyage. He whistled for Tiger to come, but the dog merely thumped his tail and made a little stir, then settled down again and closed his eyes.

Wading across the bayou with only the lantern to light his way, Jim laughed to see an old raccoon waddling along in the mud. "Tiger missed something not coming along with me," he chuckled. If there was one thing that hounds liked, it was chasing 'coons.

Pleased as he was to be sleeping at the homeplace, there was something lonesome about coming on the empty house, in the darkness. It was built no more than seven years ago, but it already looked very old, still holding to the past and brooding.

The front door had blown open, and was swinging, noisily on its hinges. And as Jim drew near, he saw something small and white sideling across the room toward him. He held his lantern high, startled at first. But then he recognized Timmie, the cat. She gave a little cry and rubbed against his legs, purring contentedly.

"So this is where you come every night," Jim said with a laugh. "You love this old place, too, don't you, and wouldn't like to see us give it up."

The cat followed Jim as he went through the two rooms. The place was almost bare, for the two brothers had let Kitty take what she needed of the furniture when she married. The black kitchen stove, that once glowed with warmth, was cold and empty now. However, in the woodbox behind it some kindling wood was left that could easily bring the warmth back again.

A ladder stood against the wall that led up to the loft which had been the room where Jim and Reuben used to sleep. It was nothing more than a home for squirrels and mice now. Jim stood still, listening to their pattering footsteps. But when he moved or when the cat made the slightest noise, there was a sudden silence.

Jim went back to the front room and spread a quilt on the floor for his bed. He kept another close by, in case the night should turn chilly. Then he blew out the lantern and drifted off to sleep, with Timmie, the cat, curled up at his feet. The mice and the squirrels began their pattering sound again, but the cat paid no attention.

Suddenly, in the darkness, Jim became aware of still another sound. It was as if someone were walking stealthily through the house. He sat up and listened closely. The wind was blowing through the chimney with a mournful sound. It rattled the shutters, and shook the branches of a spindly pin oak that had been planted close by for shade. The leaves brushed against the windowpanes like ghostly fingers scratching to be let in.

But the sound that puzzled Jim was not made by the wind. He could hear it clearly now, coming from the kitchen.

He lit his lantern and tiptoed quietly to the door. Shadows danced over the ceiling and wall, made by the flickering light. He could see nothing more. But the sound of stealthy footsteps was louder than ever. They seemed, now, to come from the direction of the front room.

He went back. He looked in all the corners and he examined the windows. They were closed, as he had left them, and the doors were still bolted.

The cat followed Jim silently, from one room to the other, and when the sound came from the front porch, she went to the door, standing with her back arched and her tail waving angrily. Suddenly there was a bark. It was Tiger! He had come after all to protect Jim while he stayed in the old house alone.

"Good old Tiger," Jim said, opening the door to let him in.

The dog came in and looked around, but would not stay. He ran out and barked again, a warning, threatening bark. Soon Jim saw a covered wagon appear on the big road in the distance, like a moving shadow. The dog stopped barking when it came in sight, and began to wag his tail, with a slow and steady thumps on the porch floor. Jim stood watching, holding the lighted lantern in his hand, wondering who could be passing this way so late in the night.

When the wagon reached the side road it came to a stop, and a voice called out more in a question than a greeting. Jim answered, and the wagon turned and came toward the house. As it drew near, he recognized William Fuller and Hewitt Puryear.

"You gave us a start all right," Mr. Fuller said when he brought the horses to a stop.

"We wondered what a light was doing here in this vacant house, and we came to see who it was staying here."

"I knew it wasn't a tramp," Mr. Puryear put in. "I said to Will, 'No tramp's going to come this way, and that's for certain. They go where there's something worth stealing.' "

"I'm sleeping here nights to make room for Jeff's folks who have come visiting," Jim replied. "Won't you come in?"

"Don't care if we do," Will Fuller said. "We're on our way home from Louisiana. Thought we'd make it on back to the farm tonight, but it's so late now a pallet would feel mighty good."

"And a little something to eat wouldn't be so bad either," Mr. Puryear put in.

Jim helped the men unhitch the horses and he dipped water from the spring nearby to pour into the trough for them. They brought in the bedding needed, and a side of venison with a frying pan to cook slices of it in.

The kitchen soon took on the warmth and coziness of a place that is lived in, with a glowing fire in the stove and the lantern shining brightly in the corners of the room.

There was a table, but no chairs, so they went out together to look for stumps of logs in

the old woodshed. Tiger followed them to the woodshed and back again into the kitchen. He lay close to the stove sniffing the wood smoke and the smell of frying venison.

Hewitt Puryear was not content with meat alone. He made fried cornbread and a pot of strong, black coffee, and they ate heartily, not knowing whether to call it supper, or breakfast at such an hour of the night. Tiger and the cat didn't bother about what to call their feast of bones. They retired to separate corners and gnawed contentedly.

As they ate, Hewitt Puryear talked about the hunting trip. They had gone as close as the wagon could make it, through the swampland down to the Gulf. There were deer there, and they had seen tracks of bears and other large animals. It had been too early for wild ducks and geese to come that far south, but there had been turkeys and quail, as many as they wanted.

"And we came across something else down there," William Fuller had been silent until then. Now he reached in his pocket and took out a small cloth sack which he opened. It was filled with grain.

"Do you know what that is?" he asked, pouring some into Jim's hand.

"It looks like rice with the hulls still on," Jim said.

"That's what it is, all right. But you'd never know it if you saw it growing in the field. I'd never seen anything like it myself, and such a sight, I'll not soon forget.

"We were down in the Cajun country, where the French refugees came a hundred and fifty years ago. You must have read about them in school. It was long before the United States was a nation but their houses, their way of farming, their talk is foreign to this day.

"And the rice fields were like a landscape from a different world—the grain as tall and lush as prairie grass, shining golden yellow in the sun. The heavy heads of rice waved like ripened wheat on the Northern prairies. I never saw such a sight and I'll never forget it!"

"I'm not likely to forget it either," Hewitt Puryear said with a laugh. "Will, here, clean forgot about hunting. We stayed at one plantation, where English was spoken, a full halfday while he looked at it and had the farmer show him everything about how the rice was grown."

"The soil there is like our own in Prairie County," Mr. Fuller interrupted. "I've a feeling, and I think I'm right about it, that whatever grows there will grow here just as well."

It would take more than planting and hoeing as they did with corn and cotton, he said. Rice must have water from the time the first green shoots came up, enough to keep the roots well covered all during the growing season.

"Some brothers named Abbott own the farm, and I learned from them about how it is done," Fuller went on. "I bought enough seed from them to plant about three acres on my own place."

He gave the little bag to Jim and told him he could keep it for himself.

"I'll show you how to hull rice," Puryear said. "It'll still be brown, but it tastes about as good as white rice that's been to the mill."

"I'd rather keep it the way it is," Jim answered, putting the sack in his pocket. "I think I'd like to try and see how it will grow here. There's a little patch of land close to the bayou where I could keep it watered."

When they had finished eating, they spread more quilts on the front room floor, to sleep the few hours until day. Tiger scratched at the door to be let out, but the cat curled up again at Jim's feet.

It seemed to Jim that he had barely time to close his eyes when he saw the sun come up, a big red ball, on the horizon. The men left without stopping to make breakfast, for they had eaten so heartily before they went to sleep, they had no appetite for more.

Jim watched them drive off in the covered wagon, away from the rising sun, until they were no more than a dot on the prairie. Then he took up the lantern so he'd have it to light his way again that night, and he started back across the bayou to his sister's home.

He whistled for Tiger, but there was no answer. He called then, and searched under the house and in the woodshed, until he gave up at last and went on without him. The dog came out to meet Jim when he arrived at the Brooks' house. He'd gone in the night to protect Jim when he thought protection was needed, but the Brooks' farm was home.

CHAPTER VI

⫸ THE YELLOW COTTON BLOSSOMS
had turned red, then formed into tight green
bolls. Now they were opening, white and
fluffy, but they were small and scattered low
on stunted stalks.

It was the first crop Jeff and Kitty had made
together since their marriage, and Jim had
helped them from the beginning. Their hopes
had been high in April when they buried the
seeds and covered them with the soft, broken
earth. Jim and Kitty had played their game
of suppose, and talked of things they'd do

84

when the cotton ripened and they had picked and sold it. Even Jeff had joined in now and then, with a slow smile that lighted up his serious face.

"We might get ourselves another cow," he said. "One of better stock than old Betsy. And maybe we could make the barn bigger when we add the room to the house."

"It would be nice to have a Graphophone like the one we hear in town when we go there. When we have our parlor," Kitty said. "I declare, it's a miracle to hear a voice come right out of a box, singing a pretty song."

Just another fatal wedding,
Just another broken heart—

She sang the tune as she chopped out sprouts of sedge grass and billygoat weeds that came up between the rows.

Jim had a small share in the crop, for the work he put in. Even in the spring he had thought of buying Trinket with the money he'd get.

"Trinket?" Kitty had exclaimed, when he mentioned it. "Why don't you get yourself a young colt?"

"I could get one, but I want Trinket," Jim answered.

"Why don't you get a bicycle? I vow I'd give a pretty, to know what it's like to ride one."

"All right. I'll get a bicycle too," Jim laughed.

Jeff had listened in silence. He, too, could find it easy to believe in miracles then, when the prairie grass was new and emerald green. The weeks passed and they saw the plants struggling up from the hard clay. The earth cracked and baked in the sun and held water like an earthen jar after every rain. They joked about the poor stand in the fields, as farmers often do. Bumblebee cotton they called it, saying it grew so low a bumblebee could stand on the ground and reach the blossoms by a little stretch of its legs.

"A bumblebee would even have to stoop to reach this cotton," Jim declared. But they still hoped that some miracle would bring in a good crop. Then, with the coming of Reuben's letter, they had counted on sending him some of the cotton money to pay his share of the farm across the bayou.

Now that the cotton was ripe and ready for picking, they put their pipedreams aside. Kitty came out to help, while old Mrs. Brooks looked after Lucy and prepared the meals for

them. Daddy Brooks insisted upon helping
in the field, and nothing Jeff and Kitty said
could keep him back.

"I had an idea this land was good when I
bought it," he said to Jeff. "The man who
sold it to me—he was a veteran same as I am,
except that he had not been to a Confederate
reunion since the war was over. He wore his
hair sort of long and wavy and had gentle
eyes. He had a railroad map showing the
whole vacant prairie. Now it's on my mind
that though you got more acres than the girls
you've got the sorriest deal."

"Now, don't you worry, Papa," Jeff answered. "We've had a bad year, that's all.
This won't keep up. Next year's bound to
be better."

"This veteran, he vowed and declared a
fellow could come here with nothing but the
clothes on his back and a good appetite. In
five years, the fellow said, you'd own a fine
house and a carriage, and a piano, too, if you
wanted one."

"We'll have them," Kitty said cheerfully.
"Just give us time. This is only the first
year."

They went up and down the rows, picking
first on one side and then the other. The

long, gray cotton sacks, dragging behind them like enormous cocoons, grew heavier and heavier with each step.

"Your mamma did such work as this, and all the plowing and planting, too, when I was off to war," Mr. Brooks said to Jeff. "And she'd card and spin the cotton as well, and weave it into cloth."

The past seemed clearer than the present to him as he told of things that happened when he fought in the Civil War.

"I was as green as the next one in the beginning of the fighting," he said. "Somebody gave the order to lie down, but I didn't hear it. All I knew, everybody had fallen on his face but me. I thought they'd all been killed and I was the only one left in the whole Confederate Army, until the fellow next to me yelled out, 'Lie down, you fool!'"

Mr. Brooks told then of the boy he had seen drummed out of the army, a gentle boy, younger than Jim even, and not ready to take up the hardships brought by war.

"I never did get his name, but I'd know him if I saw him a hundred years from now. I couldn't help feeling sorry for him, for you couldn't rightly call him a coward. He just couldn't soldier, that was all. But the older

men in the company jerked off all the buttons
from his uniform. They chased him around
in a circle with their bayonets while the
drummer boy drummed as hard as he could,
and they all sang.

*Poor old soldier! Whipped, lashed, and
driven out because he couldn't soldier.* The
old man sang a tune that was haunting. The
tune and the words stayed on in Jim's head,
even when the talk turned to more cheerful
things.

At noon, Mrs. Brooks rang the dinner bell
to call them in for the hot meal that was
waiting. They emptied their sacks on the
front porch, and the pile, there, grew higher
day by day until the last boll was picked.

Even that was little enough, compared to
the crops farmers raised in the swampland.
A bale to the acre, good land would yield; but
here on the prairie they must plant five acres
for every bale they'd have.

What had they done wrong? The same
kind of seed had been planted. And the rows
had been kept as clean as any in the swampland. How could such a little distance make
so much difference in the crop?

"Now if grass was what we wanted for a
crop, we'd have had a fine harvest," Jim said

as he looked out beyond the cottonfield to the unplowed land beyond. The tall grass, golden ripe, rippled in the breeze.

"Sedge grass makes a mighty sorry crop," Jeff replied. "There are some who cut and bale it to sell. But even a cow won't eat it if she can find something more to her liking, and a cow's none to choosy in her feeding."

Jim thought of William Fuller and the rice he planned to grow. He grew impatient to try the little handful of seed on his own place. Rice, like wheat, was a kind of grass, and grass grew well on the prairie, as Mr. Fuller had said.

"I have in mind to set out a few fruit trees," Jeff said, when the last of the cotton was picked. "If that agent comes back, after we take our cotton to market, I've a mind to buy a few apple and peach trees and see what they will do."

There was doubt in his voice, but he went on, as if to argue with himself. "Ben Lowe, up the bayou a piece, put in an orchard, that's a fact. His trees didn't grow worth shucks from the time he set them out. But Ben Lowe always was the trifling sort, leaving the work about the place for his wife and young ones to do for him."

Even as he spoke, he could look up and see
the hickory and maple saplings he had
brought from the bayou. He had planted
them beside his house for shade. They had
been planted carefully; yet they were spindly
and stunted, no taller than when they were
planted a year ago.

When all the cotton was picked and the
dry, brown stalks stripped clean of bolls, it was
loaded in the wagon to be taken to the gin
at DeVall's Bluff.

Mrs. Brooks offered to take care of the baby
so that Kitty could go along on the trip to
the county seat. She put on her white dress
with the stiff-starched angel sleeves and
bubbled with excitement on this, her first
outing since Lucy was born.

Loaded wagons from all the farms were
moving toward town and the road along the
way was sprinkled with white bits of cotton
fluff. Blown by the wind, it lay in patches
like newly fallen snow.

As they drew near DeVall's Bluff they saw
a long line of wagons waiting their turn at
the cotton gin.

"I'll stay with the load," Jeff said to Kitty.
"Why don't you and Jim take in the sights?
I'll pick you up at Gates' store. You can be

feasting your eyes on all the pretty things you want to buy."

The street from the gin house went along the bluff, past the fort.

Kitty looked hard at the spot. "Daddy Brooks'll want to hear exactly how the old fort looks," she said. "He fought a battle here when he was a soldier in the war. Likely he'll fight it all over again for us when he gets home tonight."

The way now led past houses clustered close together. And the dusty streets were filled with carriages, drays, wagons and bicycle riders.

Jim was country-born and raised and he would never get used to seeing houses built close together. It worried him to hear snatches of conversation of neighbors talking from window to window, saying things that were not meant for strangers to hear.

"He's been sparking her now for a year and a half and he's made no mention of marrying yet."

"Fifteen dollars a week's not enough to support a family on, but there are times when a man's willing to take whatever he can get."

From one house there came the blaring sound of loud music.

"That's a Graphophone, I vow!" Kitty said. Her eyes sparkled but she didn't mention wanting one, as she had in the spring.

"O zip a duden, duden, duden,
Zip a duden day."

Jim's feet kept time to the tune and he wasn't the only one. Men working at the oar factory at the foot of the bluff took up the song and whistled as they dragged in the big logs that lay floating on the river. Jim began to whistle, too, as he stopped to watch the work.

"Makin' oars for the British Navy," a man called, seeing Jim was curious. "We bring the logs from the swamp and they go journeying far away. Into other waters that wash the coast of Zanzibar, Hongkong and Bombay."

"Now, wouldn't Reuben like those names!" Kitty said.

Jim nodded—names like that brought romance and adventure to Reuben's mind. Even if he didn't know much about the places and could scarcely find them on a map, Reuben would stand in this very spot and dream.

"Reuben was always wishing he could go where the oars were going off to the corners of the earth," Jim answered. Then he laughed. "I reckon I'm just an Arkansas stay-at-home. All I was thinking about was seeing how they turn the swamp logs into oars."

He was so absorbed that he scarcely noticed when Kitty walked on, calling back that she'd be at Mr. Gates' store.

A boy Jim's age came walking along with his hands in his pockets, whistling the tune he had heard, too, from the Graphophone. Jim knew that the boy was from the country, from the way his eyes darted here and there as if they could not take in enough. Suddenly the boy stopped and stared at something across the street.

"I declare to Betsy!" he exclaimed. "Will you look over yonder way!"

Jim looked down the street and then he turned and stared at the awestruck boy.

His eyes hadn't deceived him there—that really was an angel on the steps of the Pythian Hall! A quite small angel in a long white robe, with white wings spreading wide. Jim blinked his eyes and looked again. The angel was still there with eyes turned upward and lips moving gently.

A group of old men were sitting on benches in front of the courthouse. Some were former

soldiers wearing gray uniforms that were old
and faded now, with many of the buttons
missing. They were talking among themselves, facing the Pythian Hall where the little
angel stood, but if they saw anything, they
gave no sign of it.

"Do you see it, too?" the boy asked Jim,
and ran his finger nervously along his stiff,
starched shirt collar.

"Yes," Jim answered, still not able to believe
his eyes. "Let's go take a closer look."

"Maybe we're not supposed to. Maybe we
ought not to be seeing it at all. The men
over yonder don't, for they're not paying any
attention to it," the boy replied.

But he went across the street with Jim,
easing himself as slowly and quietly as a cat
approaching a mouse. Just as they drew near,
a stout woman came to the door of the Pythian
Hall. She was wearing a flowered hat,
perched on a high topknot, and she went right
up to the angel and straightened one of her
wings. "All right, Amy," the woman said in
a loud, carrying voice, "it's about time for
your part in the play. Are you sure you can
say your lines all by heart now, without forgetting?"

"Yes Ma'am," the little angel answered as

she followed the woman inside the building.

The two boys looked at each other and burst out laughing.

"Law me," the boy said. "Just suppose we'd 'a' called out, telling folks we'd seen an angel. What country rubes they would have taken us to be!"

"Are your folks down at the cotton gin too?" Jim asked.

"Yes, and it's for the last time," the boy answered. "I'll not be coming to DeVall's Bluff again and I'll not be seeing the White River nor the prairie either after a while."

"Where are you going?"

"Back to God's country. Back to Illinois."

Jim had heard so many places called God's country, places north, east, south and west.

"It's all God's country," he answered hotly. Wherever men have loved the land there is God's country, William Fuller had said.

"Even this old prairie?" the boy asked.

"Yes, the prairie too," Jim said, believing it then with all his heart.

An old Negro man came riding by in a wagon filled with barrels and bottles of water, and he made a song as he called out to all to come and buy.

"Get your good spring water. Good Wattensaw spring water. It cures whatever ails you."

"There's better water than that old colored man's Wattensaw water right close to where I live," the boy spoke up. "LaGrue spring water. It'll cure chills and fever no matter how sick a body's been. I know, for I've tried it many a time."

"You don't say!" Jim had never seen anybody selling water before his eyes followed the old man's wagon with interest as it creaked along up the hill toward the bluff. Before it was out of sight Jeff's horse and wagon turned into the street. His wagon was emptied of its cotton. He must be through at the gin, and on his way to the store to trade!

"Good-by," Jim said to the boy, as he started to follow Jeff. "Good-by and good luck!"

When Jim came up to the hitching post in front of Mr. Gates' store Jeff was getting out of the wagon. On his face was a look of disappointment and discouragement. He knew, without being told, that the cotton had brought even less than they had expected.

"Kitty's in the store, looking at things," he said, and Jeff nodded gloomily.

When they crossed the porch and stepped

inside, Kitty was standing by the counter. Jeff's expression changed suddenly as if his discouragement were something he could wipe away with a handkerchief.

"Hello, honey," he said, smiling down at her. "Have you found something pretty to buy? Were you thinking of that taffeta for a Sunday dress?"

Kitty gave her husband a quick glance, then she turned away from a bolt of changeable silk taffeta she had been fingering.

"No," she said. "I'd look like an old lady a hundred years old wearing a dress made of it."

She bought instead some flannel for baby wrappers and a few yards of coarse cotton cloth. No word had been spoken, and yet there was an understanding among them that included even Mr. Gates, the storekeeper.

It came to Jim that thoughts could be felt, just as words were heard. It was the way of wild geese in flight or of prairie chickens who sometimes rise up in a flock together suddenly as if at a command, when none has been given. So, without any words, it was understood that nothing would be bought today except what was urgently needed.

"Before I came to America, I used to hear

such stories about it that I'd never believe were true," Mr. Gates said as he measured the cloth and cut it. He still pronounced his words with a foreign accent though he had left Germany more than forty years ago.

"I used to hear that a young man over here could do whatever kind of work he wanted to do. If he wanted to be a storekeeper, he could be a storekeeper, no matter what his father and grandfather had been before him. And I wouldn't have believed it was possible."

Jim listened in surprise.

"Do you mean you didn't have your own say about what you'd do to earn your living?" he asked.

Mr. Gates shook his head.

"I tell you it's good to live in a country that's free," he went on. "Nobody can tell me how to earn my living. Nobody can tell me how to worship. Here I choose my own business and my own church and I'm not told how to do nor what to believe. Even if times are hard, it is good to live in such a country."

They had little to say on the long ride back home. What Mr. Gates had said made them thoughtful. The freedom he had found when he first came to the prairie long ago, was something they had all accepted naturally, without giving it much thought before. But to Mr. Gates it was worth far more than all the money he had made or failed to make.

"I can do anything I want to do and be anything I want to be," Jim said to himself as they jogged along the dusty road. "If I want to be a doctor I can get a job working in Dr. Hippolite's Drug Store and earn enough money to go away to school. And if I want to be a lawyer, I can get my start in Judge Thweat's office."

Mr. Gates himself had gone about the country selling pins and needles and cloth to sew from a pack on his back, before he had a store of his own. Working hard, but doing what he wanted—because he was free.

Jim tried to picture himself a full-grown man. His mind went to first one and then the other idea. It was like trying on many suits of clothes to see how they fit, and putting each one aside.

"I'd rather keep the homeplace and farm it when I've grown man-size," he said aloud.

"Naturally," Kitty answered absently. She had picked up the weekly newspaper Jeff had bought. "Listen to this!" she suddenly exclaimed. "They've discovered gold up in the

Yukon. Isn't that where Reuben was? Pity, he left too soon."

An Indian named Skookum Jim had been the first to find the gold when he went down to the creek for water. The strike was close to where the Yukon and Klondike Rivers met, and claims were being filed at Forty Mile.

"It's the place, all right," Jim said.

"They found the gold back in August, just a couple of months after Reuben left. I wonder how he feels, reading about it now and missing a fortune by such a little bit. Oh, well," Kitty said. "He always was one to be restless. Maybe next time something big is happening, he'll be on hand. But he ought to write now and then so we'd know how he is and where."

"He won't write unless he's getting on well in his new venture," Jim replied.

"I declare, Jim. I hope when he does write, you won't change your mind and go traipsing about with him. You'd not find a nicer place in all the world than right here on the prairie, now would you?"

Jim saw a slow mile creep over Jeff's face, and the two exchanged glances but neither of them said a word. They were coming home without taffeta cloth and Graphophones. In the back of the wagon were just the most needed supplies and there was no money weighing down Jeff's pocket—but they were coming to a homeplace all of them loved.

"I saw a pretty house in town, and we could fix ours up just like it when we get around to adding that other room," Kitty was saying. "We could keep the front room as it is for the bedroom and make the new one bigger so we can use it for the parlor."

CHAPTER VII

◖ THE RAINS CAME, ONLY A FEW drops, at first, that dried as quickly as they fell. Then they poured down faster with a warm steam rising as they touched the earth. The few leaves, left clinging to the pin oak trees, opened like slender cups to hold the moisture.

There was something about the rain after a long drouth that gave a touch of spring, even in the autumn when the harvest was over. The fields were gay with asters and wild sunflowers, rising on stiff, unbending stalks above the dry grass. Early on a clear morning they were covered with spider webs, fluttering in the breeze like silk handkerchiefs spread out to dry. And, down in the grove, the gnarled old Cherokee plum put out blossoms for all the world like an old woman trying to look young.

The hard clay held the water and would not let it soak in deep, as it did in the swampland. Puddles stood in the road and the fields were like lakes, with the old dry stalks of cotton and corn reflected in the water.

Turtles came up from the bayou, and water beetles darted about. And, now and then, a water snake could be seen swimming in the flooded fields, its head showing black above the water.

There was a restlessness that comes with every change of season. Wasps flew into the house whenever the door was opened. And at the old homeplace where Jim went every night to sleep, large velvety spiders crept up between the chimney. The chimney swallows that had nested all summer in the chimney, gathered each evening, swirling and circling as if to strengthen their wings. There was a constant chatter and chirping among all the birds in the grove. Like fussy travelers, Mrs. Brooks said, getting ready to make a journey.

Blackbirds came moving in flocks to settle on the old cornstalks, eating all they could of the grain still left on. And early every morning the sky was dark with wild geese and ducks flying south.

Tiger still went at night to sleep on the porch beside Jim's door and returned to the Brooks' farm every morning early before Jim was awake. Sometimes Jim tried to coax him to go hunting in the grove, but the dog would only go a little way and then return to stand by the gate looking up and down the road.

"Dogs have queer ways the same as people," old Mr. Brooks remarked. "He misses his master."

The old man was always ready for a hunting trip. It was all Jeff or Jim could do to keep up with him when he was on the trail, stalking a deer or answering the call of a wild turkey flock. He walked with long strides and a light step as if he were as young as they.

Often, when the weather was fair, the three went off in the wagon before daybreak, to hunt in the swamps near the White River. There, they waded in high, hip boots to a quiet place to wait for the first melancholy wailing of geese flying overhead. Or they hid in the undergrowth, watching for the

flight of ducks, like waves rising and dipping and rising again.

"Never aim where they are. Aim where they're *going* to be," Mr. Brooks would whisper. He taught Jim to make the sounds of the ducks, to call them within shooting range. First a quack, soft yet clear so there would be no echo. Then a chattering call that was like the sound some fussy old mallard hen made while she fed or rested on a pond.

Jim liked to linger on in the swamps even after they had shot all the ducks and geese they needed. He knew the pintails by their graceful way of flying, and he watched the little wood ducks spread out in their flight, then ball together and spread out again.

But the mallards were his favorite of them all, with their splendid colors glistening in the sun. Sometimes they swooped down to within a few feet of where he stood, hovering over the water for a moment, then letting themselves down on the surface. But if he made the slightest move or sound, they drew up close together, then flared upward and away.

They had a way of working their wings sideways when coming down in the swamps where the tall trees grew close together. And when they rose again, they must flap their wings hard and fast.

"Did you ever notice how a duck can fly straight up or down?" Jeff's father said. "It's the only bird that can except a hummingbird."

A subscription school was started up again near Crossroads. The teacher charged a dollar a month, for there was not enough money in the county treasury for free schools that year. Jim saddled Trinket to ride to school every day with a lunch Kitty had prepared for him carried in a tin bucket.

"I declare I wish it was so you could go to the bigger school in town, but you know how it is, Jim," Kitty said to him. "Maybe next year there'll be money enough to send you."

Jim was the oldest scholar in school and tall for his age, and the teacher had him help the younger children with their lessons.

"A-B ab," the smallest ones recited in singsong. And those who had learned to read, spelled out the words Jim called from the blueback speller. "B-A ba, K-E-R ker, Baker." Their voices chimed together, shrill and loud above the sound of the older ones reciting their history or geography lessons, or reading from the McGuffey's Reader.

One day, near Thanksgiving time, a boy almost Jim's age was reading aloud: *Many young persons seem to think it of not much consequence if they do not improve their time well in youth, vainly expecting that they can make it up by diligence when they are older.* He mumbled the long words slowly to himself before he pronounced them. When he had finished reading the sentence, a girl sitting on the bench beside him took up the lesson from there. The boy put his book aside and sat staring out the window as if his mind were on other things besides Mr. McGuffey's Reader. The next day he did not return. Another family had left the prairie.

One by one, other children dropped out and moved away. Their parents were no longer able to earn their living here. At New Year's, the little one-room school had only eleven scholars. The teacher looked at the empty benches and shook his head in despair.

"This is my last year here," he said to Jim one morning before classes had commenced. He rang the bell to call the children from their play. And he counted them as they marched into the room to see who was missing that day. "From the way it looks now, there'll be no school to teach, even if I returned."

It was Friday, the day of recitations and spelling bees. The little girls wore clean starched white aprons over their calico print dresses, and the boys came with their hair brushed slick and their faces scrubbed. The children stood up before the classroom, one by one, and recited a poem learned by heart, or a speech made by some orator.

Fair stood the wind for France,
When we our sails advance,

Jim liked best the poems that told of men of old. The teacher lent him books to take home each Friday and he read them by the light of the lantern when he went to spend the night alone at the old homeplace. He read of England and of Rome and Greece in ancient times, and of the early days of his own country as well, when men left home of their birth to build a new nation where all should be free.

"And not just long ago," he said to himself. "It's happening today. People coming to America by the shipload—but not to Polka Dot Prairie. . . ."

CHAPTER VIII

☞ "IF THE TEACHER'S NOT COMING back next year, I could teach the school myself," Jim said the next morning after breakfast.

"You could, all right, but the School Board would never let you, for you're not of age," Jeff answered.

While Jim looked over the books he had brought back, Jeff read the weekly *DeVall's Bluff Enterprise*.

"This has been a good cotton year according to the paper," he said without looking up.

112

"Rain enough to get it started growing and then no rain till after the picking was over."

"Good for the folks living by the river, they mean," Kitty said with a toss of her head. "I guess that newspaperman hasn't been to the prairie—"

She wore a long, checked apron that covered her from neck to ankle, and had a towel pinned around her head. She went here and there flicking a feather duster, and when she came to the window, she stopped to look out. It was raining, and the drops were beating against the window with a moaning sound.

"Sometimes I wonder how it would feel to live in a place where it wouldn't make any difference whether the sun was shining or whether it was raining cats and dogs."

Jeff looked up from his paper, and Mr. Brooks, who was on the point of saying something, stopped with a surprised look on his face. And there was a sudden silence in the kitchen where Mrs. Brooks had been beating egg whites with a wire spoon.

Jeff and Jim loved the prairie quietly, but Kitty had always been like a mother hen whose chicks were threatened when there was talk against it. Even after they had taken the cotton to market, she could start dreaming with new hope on the return home, of the things they'd do the following year. Discouragement was something the family had not expected from her.

"The Lowes have moved away," she went on. "That's why we didn't see them at church last Sunday. The Fields have gone, too, and so have the Bakers. There's not a neighbor left for a mile on any side of us. Pretty soon we'll be the last ones living on the prairie."

She looked down at little Lucy who had learned to crawl, and was moving over the floor and getting into everything she could put her hands on.

"I vow I don't need a feather duster or a broom either, the way this child sweeps up the dirt with her dress," Kitty said as she picked her up. "Just look at these clothes, and I put them on spanking clean just a little while ago."

"Jeff, honey," Kitty went on, "I want you to make a little pen we can keep Lucy in so she won't be getting into so many things. Make one we can move about so we can take her with us out in the field when we begin our planting next spring. By then we'd never be able to keep up with her!"

Jeff smiled and put down his paper and started then and there to draw a plan on a piece of paper for a play pen.

From the kitchen there came the sound again of eggs beaten, and Mr. Brooks took up the tale he started to tell. Everybody was

happier because Kitty was her usual self, making plans for another year.

As the old man talked on about his boyhood and how he almost went to California when the gold rush was on, Jim's eyes fell on an advertisement in the paper telling how money could be made easily.

I am very young yet, and have made over $800 in ten weeks selling dish washers. It is simply wonderful how easy it is to sell them. For the benefit of others, I will state that I got my start from the Mound City Dish Washer Co., St. Louis. Write to them and they will give you full particulars.

Jim took the writing tablet and inkwell and pen back to the old homeplace with him that night, and wrote letters in answer to advertisements wanting men to sell dish washers, and lightning churns, a special kind of lamp wick, a self-heating flatiron.

On Monday morning on his way to school, he mailed the letters at the Crossroads post office.

Each school day after that, he stopped off to see if there was any mail for him. It was too cold now for the men to gather in groups on the porch, so they sat inside around the pot-bellied iron stove. Mrs. Gilpin was always there, too, in her usual chair by the window, close enough to listen to the talk of the men, but far enough away so that she was not part of the group. And she worked endlessly on her sewing.

The men talked now of the cold and rain instead of the heat and drouth. The elections were over. Mr. McKinley was elected President and they were no longer interested in politics. They argued, instead, about people moving away and what those who were staying on had planned to do.

The name of William Fuller came up often, and Jim listened eagerly to any news of him. Since the night in late summer when he had stopped by on their way home from the hunting trip, Jim had thought often of the serious-eyed, round, little man.

"He's a queer one all right," one of the men said. "You can't get within shouting distance of him before he starts all that talk about rice. Rice, rice, rice. It's all you hear from morning till night when he's around."

"Did you see that contraption he's putting in for a well?" another laughed. "He's bought some kind of wood-burning pump. Claims he's going to flood three acres of his farm this summer and grow rice on it, to prove this prairie is good for something."

"He'd better stick to baling sedge grass for hay," Mr. Gilpin joined in. "Whoever heard of growing crops under water! Look what happens in time of high water over in the swamps, when the fields are all flooded. Everything's dead by the time the water goes down."

Mrs. Gilpin looked up from her sewing and nodded approval at her husband's words, but she said nothing.

Letters finally began to come in for Jim. But they were not the kind he had hoped for. Several offered him jobs without asking questions about his age and experience. But they required that he pay money he didn't have for samples of the goods to be sold.

At first the men in the post office stopped their talk and waited in curiosity to know what the letters were about. But soon they lost interest when there were so many alike. Finally Jim began putting them in his pocket unopened.

"Well, I reckon that's one way to get mail," one of the men said with a laugh.

"The trouble is, I get paid for the ones going out, and not a cent on the ones coming in," Mr. Gilpin answered.

There was one letter with a postmark which Jim could not read because it was smeared and blotted. He put it in his pocket unopened with the rest but that night at home when he opened it, he saw that it was from Reuben.

Dear Sister Kitty and Brothers Jeff and Jim—

The letter as usual, in Reuben's big brother way, hoped Kitty and Jeff were happy, and told Jim to mind his manners.

You'll be surprised to learn I've come on to New York, when the last time I wrote I was going to Chicago. Well, I stayed in that city just long enough to see there wasn't any future in those horseless carriages.

Maybe I'm wrong, but it seems to me they're nothing but rich sportsman's toys to ride around in on paved city streets. They'll bog down in the mud worse than any wagon and it takes two strong mules to pull one out.

Besides, I figure it's a lot cheaper to buy oats for a horse than gasoline for a horseless carriage. And you can depend

on a horse and raise stock from it. But a
machine just wears out in the end and
that's all there is to it. Even if I had
money I wouldn't put it in that contraption.

However, Reuben must have some scheme
to believe in, something that would make his
fortune. When he gave up one, there was
always another to take its place. This time
he had heard about pictures that moved right
before your eyes as if the places and the people
in them were real. He had even seen one,
of a train that came closer and closer until it
seemed on the point of running over the whole
audience. Women screamed and strong men
held onto the arms of their chairs.

It was like Reuben to want to go to a place
outside of New York where such pictures were
being made, just to see how it was done. But
he needed money, and again he asked if the
farm had been sold.

If you haven't found a buyer, then
sell Trinket for whatever you can get.
That old mare's not worth keeping much
longer. I'll take as little as twenty-five
dollars for her. I'm going to need all I
can put my hands on to help me get a
start here. But the future is bright. I

tell you, big things are happening in this world.

"Well, Jim, what will we do now?" Kitty asked.

"I'll buy Trinket for myself," Jim answered grimly.

"Yes, that's what you said before, but how are you going to do it?"

"I'll think of a way. Trinket and I will earn it together, somehow."

He had said that, too, before, and at the time it had seemed easy enough. But something had to be done now, and he could waste no more time just thinking about it. The jobs offered in the advertisements were of no help, for he could no more pay for the samples than he could pay for Trinket. There must be something else.

Once he might have hired out to some other farmer, but the few that stayed on were not earning enough to have extra help.

"You can help, I know, Trinket," he said to her when she came up to drink. "But how?"

The memory of that day they had gone to the cotton gin came back to Jim when he looked out over the field of brown stubble. He thought of the disappointment each of them had felt and tried to hide from the other.

Jim could see old Mr. Gates in his store, and the old men sitting on the courthouse grounds, and the little girl who took the part of an angel in a play. He thought of the country boy, who was so sure he saw a real angel, and of the man passing by in his wagon selling Wattensaw Spring water.

"There's better water than Wattensaw right close to where I live." The boy's words came back to Jim.

He stopped suddenly in his chores and saddled Trinket. It was water from LaGrue Spring that boy talked about. Jim decided to ride off to the LaGrue Springs and see for himself what it was like. As he drew near, he saw a house with smoke coming from the chimney, a rare sight on the prairie these days. And at the spring he found a man busy filling bottles and barrels.

"Howdy," the man greeted him. "How'd you like a drink of the best water in the world?"

He filled a tin cup and gave it to Jim to drink, telling him all the while of how good it was and the way it could cure chills and fever.

"Now you take Hot Springs and Eureka

Springs and the Sugar Loaf. Folks go from all over the country just to take the water cure in those places. But a fellow here in Prairie County wouldn't have to leave his front door to drink water just as good and a little bit better."

Jim knew that in some places where the land lay low, the water was not always good. In dry weather the creeks and wells were low and sluggish and filled with dirt and fallen leaves. And after heavy rains when the water overflowed, people who drank from the wells sometimes took sick. The farmers who lived in the swampland drank bottled water from pure springs when they could.

"Do you need someone to help you sell it?" Jim asked.

"No," the man answered. "I have as many coming here to buy on the place as I can supply."

He gave a bottle of the water to Jim to take home with him, and said he'd like to have him for a customer.

"Yes, I know the LaGrue water," old Mr. Brooks said, when he took a sip from the glass Jim offered him. "It's good, and so is the Wattensaw water good. But they won't hold a candle to the springs you've got right on your own place, Jim, right across the bayou."

"You mean the springs close to the house?" Jim asked in surprise. "Why, that's nothing but plain water."

"It may be plain but it's pure and good-tasting as well. When I was young and living in the swampland over yonder, I used to ride out of my way to get a drink of that water. Remembering it made me ready to listen to the man who sold me Jeff's acres. It was the thing I recollected most about the prairie!"

Jim filled his bucket that night when he went to the old homeplace to sleep. He drank the water as if it were something he had never had before. It *did* have a good taste, not hard nor bitter like some water.

"It's a funny thing," he said to himself, "to have someone else tell me about my own spring. But I reckon you get used to your own and don't notice the difference."

Next morning, he raked away the grass that grew close and dug the loose dirt away from the bubbling springs. When the water flowed clean and clear, he borrowed some bottles from Kitty. He filled these to take for samples.

He'd been so busy with his project for selling spring water that he hadn't paid attention to what was going on at Jeff's house. When he came across the bayou with his saddlebags filled with bottles of water, he found Mr. and Mrs. Brooks ready to leave.

"Sally and her family will have been looking for us long ago," Mrs. Brooks said. "We're made to feel so much at home wherever we go, it's hard to leave."

But, now, she was bonneted and gloved, primly waiting to be helped into the buggy by her husband. And the portmanteau and carpetbag were in the buggy.

Jim fastened his saddlebags to Trinket's saddle and rode beside the buggy to see the old people on their way. Mr. and Mrs. Brooks sat sedately with the wind blowing against their faces, but it was all Trinket could do to keep up with their spirited, young, dapple-gray horse.

At the Indian mounds where the road made a turn, he got off the horse to say good-by. He stood waiting until the buggy was far in the distance. He'd miss the old couple, he knew, as much as Jeff and Kitty would.

No one else could point out tracks in the mud the way the old man could. Hunting would not be nearly so much fun alone, or even with Jeff along. Old Mr. Brooks could follow the footprints of an opossum from a woodpile to a hole in the stump of a tree. And he knew from the way a deer's sharp-pointed hoofs had marked the earth how big it was and how long ago it had passed by.

Jim sat down on the sunny side of one of the mounds, holding Trinket's reins in his hands. A small, gray rock lay at his feet, and when he picked it up he saw by its queer shape that it was an arrowhead, carved by Indians of long ago. Such a small thing as that would have started Mr. Brooks off on some story of Indians he had known back when he was a boy. And he'd have a way of making it seem as if it were only yesterday, in the telling.

"You can talk about thieving, scoundrel Indians all you want, but the ones I knew were for all the world like other folks," he had once said. "Oh, now and then, you'd find a tramp among them that took to the woods, the same as with other people. But most of them had stout log houses, and peach orchards and barnyard animals."

The old man remembered the march of the Cherokees along the military road that led through Arkansas. They were driven from their homes in Alabama and Tennessee and Georgia, because the land they claimed as their own was coveted by others.

Mr. Brooks said he was only a child then. But when he told about the way they passed, tired and hungry and many of them sick, on their way to a land they did not know, you'd think it happened yesterday.

"I was a little fellow still in dresses, the kind a child then had to wear. But since that day I could never bring myself to hate an Indian," the old man had said. "And when they talk about Sitting Bull and the Apaches on the warpath, I get to thinking about those other Indians on their way to the Oklahoma Territory."

Jim wondered what had happened to the Indians who had made these mounds that rose higher than a house. Had they been driven off by some stronger tribe and marched away as the Cherokees were? Or had they abandoned the land themselves, as the prairie farmers were doing now?

There must have been old camp sites once, empty and haunted-looking as his own house and the others, that stood deserted on the prairie. Would these houses crumble, too, and become a part of the earth? With prairie grass growing over every trace of them, as it did over the old camp sites?

A feeling of impatience came over Jim. As

if the houses and land, the whole prairie, depended on him, he jumped to his feet. He mounted to ride as fast as Trinket would take him, to the lowland near Bayou Meto to sell his spring water.

When he came to a farmhouse, he called out. A young man opened the door. Jim took one of the sample bottles of spring water with him, but once inside the house he couldn't think of anything to say. All the things he had thought of on the way left him. He could only pass the time of day, talking about such things as the last big rain and the way the water stood in the fields like acres of lakes, and of the signs of an early spring.

The man's wife and children sat in the room and looked on silently while the man talked in neighborly fashion with Jim.

"What's that you have in your hand? Is it water you're selling?" the man asked at last.

"Yes, sir, it's pure spring water, and it's as good as any water you'll find at Hot Springs or any other place where people go for their health," Jim answered. The words came with a rush now and his shyness was forgotten. "I can bring it to you once every week, and if you drink it all winter, there'll be no need to take a tonic in the spring."

"Will it cure chills and fever?" the wife spoke up.

Jim hesitated. That was the claim they made for Wattensaw water and LaGrue water. Chills and fever were the besetting illness of those who lived near the swamps. The medicine men that went about the country selling their cures often had nothing more than colored spring water which they claimed would cure every known ailment.

Jim felt the woman's eyes upon him, waiting for his answer. She was plump, with cheeks as red as apples. Her husband looked strong and healthy, too, and their two small children looked as if they were never sick a day in their lives. They had stopped in their play and stood staring, too, at him.

"Bad water makes you sick, and clean, pure water will keep you in good health," Jim found himself saying. "But I couldn't say for sure that any water's going to cure you of something you've already got."

He started to turn and go back to his horse but the man called him back. He and his wife were laughing, and the children joined in, though they seemed not to be sure just why.

"Come back, young fellow," the man said.

"We wanted to find out first if you were honest. We need bottled water all right. The Bayou Meto is muddy and none too fit to drink, and we've been boiling every drop we've used. I've held off buying water till now for we won't buy from anybody making claims we know are not so."

He gave Jim an order for a barrel of spring water to be delivered every week. Then he told of others living near who might buy also, for there were no springs for miles around.

"Little old Trinket," Jim said as they rode home after sundown. "There'll be no more talk about selling you from now on."

He'd have to have a name for his water, but what could it be? All the way home he tried to think of one, and then, when he saw the old homestead in the distance, like a dot on the prairie, it came to him.

"Polka Dot Prairie Spring Water," he said. "It's a long name, but that's what I'll call it." He said it over and over to himself to get used to the sound. *Polka Dot Prairie Spring Water, sold by James Luckett and his partner, Trinket.*

CHAPTER IX

☞ JIM DIVIDED HIS TIME BETWEEN school and peddling water for the next three months. He brought as many old barrels as he could from the Crossroads store, and when he needed still more, he went to the stores of DeVall's Bluff. With Kitty's help the barrels were scalded and scrubbed and made as fresh and clean as new.

Every Saturday morning, before the sun came over the horizon, Jim filled them with sparkling clear water from his springs, and he rode with them in the back of the wagon, along the prairie roads.

Before the winter was over, Polka Dot Spring Water became as well known as LaGrue or Wattensaw water, and some who drank it made claims for its power to cure that Jim would never have thought about.

With the first money he earned, he built a wall around the springs and sank a pipe deep down for the water to come through so it could be kept pure. And after that was done, he put every cent he earned in a jar which he kept in the loft, to save until there was enough to pay Reuben for Trinket.

"Where will you send it?" Kitty asked, as the jar began to fill. "There's no telling where Reuben is now. He's such a rolling stone."

"It does look like he'd write us once in a while," Jim answered. "Anyhow, next time we hear where he is, I'll have the money to buy Trinket."

On weekdays, until the subscription school closed, Jim delivered the water to places close to his home or on the way to Crossroads. But when the teacher had gone and school was out, he went out beyond Prairie County, into the next county as well.

He rode past William Fuller's farm once a week and delivered water there. Mr. Fuller could hardly wait for springtime to try out his rice. He had dug a well and put in a pump. Jim saw the pump tried out one day and it really worked. With the first faint hint of spring, Mr. Fuller began plowing his land and building the terraces to hold the water.

"I'll have to get busy on my own land," Jim said, when he saw what had been done. "I haven't even started on it."

Mr. Fuller smiled. "Do you still have that seed I gave you last year?" he asked.

"Yes, and I've been wondering when it ought to be planted."

"You'll have to wait till cotton planting time, sometime in April or early May, for rice needs a warm earth to make it sprout. It's a hot weather plant," Mr. Fuller said. "But make sure you have your levees built up in time, for this crop needs to be kept under water from the time it's three weeks out of the ground."

The February snow had scarcely melted when the swollen leafbuds began to burst, giving a tawny rust color to the island grove. And the maples came out with splashes of red. The Carolina wrens had sung feebly all winter. Now, they began to raise their voices a little higher, and here and there a nest was built in the fork of a bare tree. It was like peering into someone's window or open door to see the nests unhidden by leaves.

Jim started then to prepare his soil for his own little handful of seeds. He turned it over with a spade and crumbled the hard, stubborn clods between his hands to make it finer still. Then he built up a mound of earth a few inches high around it to hold the water when it was needed.

The wild ducks came again, and the first frogs began croaking near the bayou. May apples sprang up like little green umbrellas slowly opening, and wild violets bloomed in shady places in the grove.

At the few farms where there were people staying on, fields were newly plowed, ready to receive the seed for another crop. And in the abandoned places, the dry sedge grass gave way to tender green shoots that sprouted up tall enough to hide the creatures nesting beneath.

Sometimes, in early morning, Jim could hear a booming sound like Indian drums beating, and he knew it was the mating call of the prairie cocks. Somewhere, hidden in the grass, they were stepping and prancing like Indians in a dance, with their feathers ruffled like war bonnets blowing in the wind. There were the Indian paintbrushes blooming on the prairie, and the star-like Indian pinks also. The blue sweet williams and spiderwort, and the yellow Spanish needles and black-eyed Susans began to bloom. It was as if a gaily-colored Indian blanket had been spread over the earth.

When the oak leaves grew to the size of a mouse's ear and the mourning doves called from the grove and all danger of frost was over, the farmers began to plant their hot weather crops. Cotton was planted in even rows and corn in hills three feet apart. It was then that Mr. Fuller sowed his rice.

When Jim came by with his water barrels and saw the terraced fields so neatly sown, he wanted to turn right back and plant his own patch. And the next day he was up before dawn planting his seed on the homeplace.

"Anything grows well this time of year," the farmers said when they saw the rice in Mr. Fuller's field, as green as new prairie grass, with blades that were as sturdy. "Wait and see what happens in the summer heat and drouth."

They pointed to their own fields, with plants as green and healthy and they talked

of other springs when their hopes were high
and of the disappointment that came with the
summer and the fall.

Even with Mr. and Mrs. Brooks gone, Jim
slept often at the farm across the bayou—"his
own place" he called it to himself—though of
course it belonged to Reuben and Kitty, too.
Tiger went along every night, like a shadow
that followed behind without ever catching
up. He curled up beside the front door, and
stayed until early dawn. Then he went
quietly back across the bayou without even a
parting bark.

Jim cultivated some more of the land on
the far side of the slope. He plowed under
the sedge grass and in its place he planted
oats. That, too, was a kind of grass, and
should do well on prairie soil. And Jeff put
in a few fruit trees which he had bought when
the agent came back that way. Springtime
and hoping went together.

It was a time for experimenting among the
farmers that were left on the prairie. Some
tried sugarcane for sugar, and others put in
ribbon cane or sorghum for molasses. Tobacco was planted and wheat was tried again.

But springtime passed and the summer grew
hot and cloudless as it had the year before.

The wheat and tobacco withered; the cotton was stunted and dry before it had time to reach its full growth.

Jim filled the little patch beside the bayou with water which he brought by the bucketful, and he saw the rice come up above it, as rich green in color and strong and sturdy as in the spring. But the oats he planted had not even tried to break through the hard, blue clay.

When their own crops were laid by, with the hoeing and weeding over and the little to be harvested not yet ready, the neighboring farmers gathered at William Fuller's farm. They saw the stalks rise tall above the water. They stared at the green stalks reflected in the water and at the grains, like dainty tassels at the top, beginning to form. They watched the crude little pump as it chugged to bring up the water and pour it out over the field.

The tall, gaunt men who had had so many disappointments still shook their heads and said the crop would not live to be harvested. But even as they said it, they were eager to be proved wrong. And in spite of all they said a gleam of hope showed in their faces.

One morning when Jim was driving by, the chugging of the pump stopped. Mr. Fuller rushed out, splashing through the water in his rubber boots, and Jim tagged along behind him.

"What is it?" he asked. "What went wrong?"

The noise of the pump had become part of the prairie, like the wind or singing birds. When it stopped, the silence drifted out over the land and neighbors put down their own work and came across the fields anxious to know what the trouble was.

They offered Mr. Fuller advice as he tried one thing and then another, and still the pump would not go. At last, in his haste to repair it, William Fuller gave a quick, impatient tug and the pump came apart in his hands. It was broken now for good and all, and no amount of tinkering could put it together again.

Next week, when Jim brought the barrel of spring water, he saw that the water in the rice field had disappeared. The earth had become as dry and hard as on all the other prairie farms. And the rice, like the corn and cotton, was slowly withering.

There were some among the farmers who said, "I told you so." But the words were not spoken in triumph, for their hopes had gone,

said. "You're going to put it in a sack so weavils can't get in it and you're going to plant it next year."

"Next year," Jim echoed. "There won't be any next year. Mr. Fuller's gone away. He's left the prairie. His ground is baked and the rice stalks are dry. If *he* couldn't make rice grow that proves the land is fit for nothing but sedge grass. When Reuben writes again, I guess I might as well give up and go where he's gone."

"But, honey, your rice grew," Kitty said with a quaver in her voice.

Without answering, Jim put the bag of grain away and went out to help Jeff pick cotton. For the next few days Kitty and Jeff and Jim were busy harvesting the small crop. They talked about old Mr. and Mrs. Brooks who had been with them last harvest time. But they didn't talk about adding rooms to the house or buying books or Graphophones as they had last year. What was there to say?

When all the cotton was gathered, Jeff hitched up the wagon and they set off for the cotton gin. Lucy came along so the wagon seat was crowded and Jim saddled Trinket and rode ahead. The streets of DeVall's Bluff were almost empty. Many of the shops and stores were vacant. There was gloom on the faces of the farmers and the merchants as well.

It was not only the drouth and the sorry crops that weighed on their spirits but the war they were sure would come. Spain and Cuba and the Philippines were names on every tongue. And the question was asked over and over, "How soon will it be before we're in it, too?"

When they were ready to return home, Jim lifted Lucy up on the saddle to ride with him. It seemed to him as if the horse stepped more lightly these days—as if she knew there was money saved to keep her from being sold to a stranger. Jim would not need to take any of the money from the cotton. Polka Dot Spring Water had earned enough.

"Trinket and I—we're partners," Jim said to Lucy as they trotted along the hard-baked road.

Lucy clutched a china doll he had bought her and she chattered like a little monkey as they rode along. The words had no meaning to anyone but herself, but now and then she broke into a merry laugh.

"Sounds like she's saying 'Cuba and the Philippines,'" Jim called back.

Cuba and the Philippines had been nothing more than colored places on the map before, but they were brought closer every week when the *DeVall's Bluff Enterprise* was brought home from the Crossroads.

"There's something in the air," Mr. Brooks said, when they came a few weeks later for their annual visit. "I'd know it even if I never read a newspaper myself. It was this way just before Fort Sumter was fired on back in '61. Something's going to happen again, just as sure as you're born."

CHAPTER X

TWO THINGS HAPPENED DURING
the visit of the old couple. The American
battleship, Maine, was blown up in the harbor
of Havana. This brought the war with Spain
closer than ever.

"Remember the Maine!" The cry went up
all over the country, from New York to California, and in all the lonesome settlements
between.

The other thing that happened was
Reuben's return home. He had not written
he was coming, and appeared suddenly riding
down the road on a horse he had hired from

the livery stable at DeVall's Bluff. No one recognized him at first. Even the dog, Tiger, who had grieved for so long for his absent master, ran out and barked threateningly, as to a stranger.

Jim glanced out of the window at the man in city clothes who, nevertheless, rode a horse as if he were used to riding. "It's Reuben coming," Jim shouted as he dashed out the door.

He saw his brother get down from the horse and hitch it to the gate post, and then stretch out his hand to the barking dog.

"Tiger, old fellow. What's the matter? Don't you know me?"

The dog recognized his voice and hung his head, the picture of shame. He tried to tuck his tail and wag it at the same time, and when he saw Jim come running down the path, he went up to stand beside him, as if he knew no other master.

"He didn't know you, Reuben," Jim said. "I had to take a second look myself before I was sure it was you."

The two brothers shook hands, and clapped each other on the back, but as they walked together to the house, they stole quick glances at each other, as strangers do who are only beginning to get acquainted. They smiled and talked of ordinary things, trying to pretend there had been no long separation.

"I didn't expect to find you grown to man size when I came home," Reuben said. "You've changed a lot. I doubt if I'd have known you if I'd met you on the street in town."

But to Jim it seemed that Reuben was the one who had changed. He must surely have grown shorter. When he went away, Reuben had towered above him, and now Jim was the taller, and could look down on his older brother.

"Reuben Luckett, as I live and breathe," Kitty said as she came out on the porch to meet him. She threw her arms around him laughing and scolding at the same time because he had not written. "Why in the world don't you let a person know you're coming? We'd have fixed up a little more for you."

With Kitty bustling about, the shyness of the first meeting between the two brothers wore away. Soon Jeff's parents were talking, too, everyone eagerly asking questions about the places Reuben had been—the wonders he had seen.

Jim wanted to know about the pictures that

moved, but Reuben only shook his head and answered, "They're nothing but a fad. A sort of toy. People will soon lose interest in them."

It was the same when Mrs. Brooks asked about the horseless carriages. "Only a fad, a sort of toy," Reuben said.

And the questions about the West, about gold mines in Alaska were answered with a shrug.

"Well, I hope you'll give up traipsing around now, Reuben, and settle down here where you belong," Kitty said.

"No," Reuben answered, smiling down at her for her seriousness. "I've come back here to see you folks and say good-by again. There's going to be war, and it won't be long in coming. And when it does, I'll be in it."

Jim expected Reuben to talk again of selling the homeplace, but nothing was said about it. Instead, Reuben had a way of walking over the farm, examining every corner as an old friend paying a call after a long absence.

The first day, Tiger started after him, then turned back to see if Jim were coming. When he did not, the dog looked from one to the other and hesitated, as if trying to make up his mind. Then he turned and stayed behind with him.

"It looks like the dog as well as the horse is yours," Reuben said.

"He's getting old, that's all," Jim answered. "He hasn't followed me even when I'd start off with my gun to hunt."

But the dog followed Jim down to the spring and back to the wagon as he brought water to fill his barrels. Reuben stood alone on a slope where the land rose gently and called back to Jim.

"What's this green stuff growing over in the far corner there?" he asked.

"It couldn't be prairie grass this time of year," Jim said, going to join his brother.

It had been a long time since Jim had been over the whole two hundred acres, for the days were growing short, edging toward autumn, and there was little enough daylight left when he returned in the evening after delivering the spring water. The last time he had gone beyond the slope, the whole place had been covered with snow. Now, as he looked, he saw a field of bright green, as if that one small spot had captured the spring and held it fast.

"Why, that's where I planted the oats," Jim said, in surprise. He ran up the slope and picked one of the stalks to examine it. "It is oats for sure! I planted them late in the

spring and they didn't even come up except in
ragged patches. Now look at them, growing
as thick as sedge grass in the fields."

Rice in summer and oats in winter! What
a place this would be if they could grow these
two things! Reuben listened silently when
Jim told him about William Fuller's experi-
ment, and about his own little bed of rice.

"I've got enough seed to plant a larger field
of it next spring," Jim said, forgetting what a
hard time Kitty had had to keep him from
throwing the rice away.

"And is he going to plant more of it, too?"
Reuben asked. "Mr. Fuller, I mean."

Jim shook his head. "No, he's gone away,
and he's the last person in the world I'd ever
think would leave the prairie."

Something of Reuben's old restlessness and
impatience with the prairie came back then.

"Like I said before," he said. "A fellow
can't get anywhere staying on here. When
I come back from the war, you and I will go
off together somewhere. We'll sell this place
and make our way in the world."

But even as he spoke, there was something
about the way he looked out over the land,
that showed the affection he felt for it. "It's
too bad," he added slowly. "But that's the

way it is. And there's big things happening
out there."

He helped Jim fill the barrels with water
and even rode with him in the wagon when
he made the deliveries. Often, through the
winter, they went far enough from home to
stay overnight, stopping at some farmhouse
along the way, where they were made welcome. And each time they returned, Reuben's
eyes searched the horizon until the first faint
glimpse of their home appeared, a dark spot
in the distance. Then he seemed to settle
back with something of a smile of satisfaction.
Even after Jeff's parents finished their visit
and went away, Reuben and Jim stayed on in
the homeplace.

Jim had paid the money for Trinket soon
after Reuben's return. But one day in spring,
Reuben gave him back the twenty-five dollars
with some more money added.

"You keep this for me, Jim," he said. "I
won't be needing any money where I'm
going."

In April, war was declared, and Reuben
packed a small hand satchel to be on his way.

"I'm going now," he said. "I'll take the
train at DeVall's Bluff and go from there to
Little Rock where I'll volunteer."

"I'm going too," Jim announced. "I'm big enough to go in the army."

He stood beside Reuben, with his head towering above that of his older brother, as he spoke.

"Jim Luckett, the very idea!" Kitty spoke up. "I won't have you even talking about such a thing!"

"It's not for you or Jim either to decide that," Jeff said quietly. "They're not taking volunteers under eighteen years old in this war."

"Then I'll go on the train as far as Little Rock," Jim said. "At least I can see Reuben off to the fighting."

"I'll write a letter to sister Millie right away," Jeff said. "She lives right in town and she'll want you both to stay with her while you're there. And it wouldn't surprise me if you find the folks are there. When Papa finds out there's going to be a parade to see the soldiers off, he'll not want to miss it for the world."

*   *   *

Jim had not ridden on a train since they first came to the prairie, when he was a small boy. It had seemed strange to be going away without saddling Trinket, or hitching her to the wagon or to Jeff's buggy, but once they were on the train he felt ready to ride forever.

The rolling wheels made a sound like voices singing, sometimes shrill and high, with now and then a deep bass note chiming in. Jim could even imagine he heard the words as he sat beside the window looking out at the ever-changing landscape. And he hummed the tune of a song that had been going through his head.

When Johnny comes marching home again,
Hooray! Hooray!

The wheels clanked out in merry rhythm, "Hooray, hooray, hooray." And the oil lamp over head, swinging on its brass chain, seemed to be keeping time, with the voices of the passengers droning a soft accompaniment.

The plume of black smoke trailing from the engine rose up and lost itself in the darkening sky. The shadows grew long, giving an air of mystery to the landscape outside.

It was easy then to imagine that the train was standing still and the trees themselves were gliding past. They were like giants dancing with outstretched arms to the rhythm of the wheels.

When the conductor came through to light

the lamp, it was as if a thin black curtain had been drawn suddenly across the window, shutting out the view. Jim could see his own reflection looking back at him. He seemed to be on the outside, floating along beside the train, as well as inside looking on.

The newsbutch came down the aisle with his basket on his arm, calling out in a sing-song voice:

Peanuts, popcorn, apples, candy.

Peanuts, popcorn, apples, candy.

Reuben bought two apples and Jim opened the shoe box which Kitty had filled with good things to eat: fried chicken and jelly cake and hardboiled eggs and pickles.

Soon after they had finished eating, the train gave a long, mournful whistle, then pulled to a stop at Little Rock.

A crowd of people stood waiting at the station platform, some to get on the train to go farther south, others to meet passengers coming in. But it seemed to Jim that many had come only in idle curiosity to watch the trains pass by.

"Jim! Reuben!"

It was strange to hear their names called out from such a crowd. As they stepped down from the cars Jim saw someone jostling his way to the front of the platform. It was old Mr. Brooks.

Jeff was right. When there was a promise of seeing soldiers the old man could not be kept away. He had heard, besides, that there would be a Confederate Reunion, with the old soldiers marching in the parade beside the young ones going off to war. He was dressed even now in his gray uniform, neatly pressed, with the buttons polished until they sparkled.

"This is Millie's husband," Mr. Brooks said, introducing a pleasant-faced man in a blue suit. "We got Jeff's letter and came to fetch you to the house to stay. Kind of different from the open prairie," the old man went on, as they pushed through the crowd onto the sidewalk paved with bricks.

Jim turned back for a last look at the train standing at the station, its engine puffing, impatient to be off again. Another train of freight cars went rumbling past on the curving track beyond.

Once Reuben would have stopped to watch it, too, wishing that he were going on, wherever it was headed for. But, now, he walked straight ahead staring down the crowded street—past the tall, brick buildings, and the mule-drawn drays. Reuben was not even noticing the crowds of men and women, dark-skinned and white. He had only one thing on his mind.

"Where's the recruiting office?" he asked.

Reuben volunteered at the recruiting office. Then he and Jim saw the sights of town together while they waited for the time Reuben must leave.

"Was it like this in the cities you saw in the North?" Jim asked Reuben, time and again.

"Yes, just about like this," Reuben replied. "Only the buildings are taller and the crowds are bigger, that's all. And there are electric cars and elevated railways—and, in the seaports like New York and Seattle, the ocean liners. But places and people are not much different when you get right down to knowing them."

They went to a penny arcade where Jim looked inside a box and saw pictures moving before his eyes as he turned a crank. Somewhere in the room a Graphophone with a horn like a big morning-glory played the latest ragtime music. It was all they could do to keep from dancing a jig then and there.

The day came when the newly-recruited soldiers must take their leave. They marched in a parade down Main Street, then turned toward the railroad station. Flags were flying and banners waving. The bands played, with drums beating loudly.

Jim walked along the sidewalk, following the parade, and he tried to keep Reuben in sight. The recruits were still dressed in their ordinary clothes, but they held their heads high and in their eyes there was a look of adventure. Yet it seemed to Jim that there was a look of homesickness, too, for the place they were leaving behind. Behind the volunteers going to a new war, marched the old soldiers in their bluish-gray uniforms. Now and then there was a grayish-blue uniform of a Northern soldier who had come to live in the South.

Reuben and his companions boarded the train that was waiting at the station for them, and the crowds stood to watch the line of cars glide onto the ferry to cross the river.

Jim was standing next to old Mr. Brooks but they had little to say to each other. Each was busy with his own thoughts—the one remembering a war long past, and the other wondering why the army wouldn't take a big strapping boy even if he hadn't turned eighteen.

CHAPTER XI

☛ JIM WENT BACK ON THE TRAIN alone. Even with Reuben gone, he decided to stay on at his old homeplace. He mended the barnyard fence and kept Trinket and Tiger there with him. He was not lonely because Jeff and Kitty spent as much time with Jim as they did at their own home. There was so much going back and forth that a regular path was tramped out down to both banks of the bayou.

Jeff and Jim worked together cutting down trees from the grove to make furniture for the two rooms. They made a bed with logs for the posts, and Kitty stuffed a mattress with goose feathers to go on it. They made benches, too, with smaller logs for legs, and wide split logs for the tops.

The house no longer had that deserted, haunted look, now, with a dog to guard it and smoke coming from the chimney. And in late spring Jim plowed and terraced a patch of ground close to the bayou and planted the rice. Soon this was green with newly sprouted grain.

Jim put a mailbox at his gate, for now there was the new Rural Free Delivery and he no longer had to ride off to the Crossroads post office for the mail.

The weekly newspaper was delivered, bringing news about Commodore Dewey and the way the Spanish fleet was destroyed. There wasn't a farmhouse on the prairie that didn't know of young Theodore Roosevelt and his Rough Riders at El Caney and General Kent on San Juan Hill.

They read of battles fought and won in other places too. Cuba. The Philippines. Puerto Rico. Jim could see these places in his mind, with hills and forests, and men fighting. And somewhere among them was Reuben.

Jim pictured his brother in every place that

was mentioned—in every battle, until at last there came a letter from halfway across the world, in the Philippines.

After the first letter, one or two more came with the strange-looking postmark. Reuben's letters didn't say much but they meant more to Jim and Kitty than all the thousands of printed words in the newspaper. It was "Reuben's war" to them and when, three months later, news of victory came it was Reuben's victory.

Jim's field of rice had grown tall and begun to ripen. He could never have kept so much land under water if Jeff and Kitty had not worked with him. Whatever time they could spare from the cotton, they spent helping with the patch of rice.

The fruit trees Jeff had planted so hopefully had died. But he could look with pride on the little patch of rice rising as healthy and tall above the water this year as the last. On sunny days the sun sparkled over it, with the green and blue of stalks and sky mirrored below.

The rice had become something of a symbol to them all. If the stalks began to droop the least bit, they worked together digging a deep ditch to bring in water from the bayou. And when a high wind bent the rice low and twisted it in bunches so that they thought it would never rise again, their own hopes fell with it. When the sun came out, it lifted their spirits as it lifted the rice heads.

"I declare, Jim, this patch is about the prettiest thing on the whole prairie," Kitty said. "But it takes a lot of work to keep it this way."

Often when Jim came back from delivering the spring water, he would find Jeff and Kitty in his field, wading with rubber boots, while little Lucy splashed barefoot beside them. They pulled up by hand the wild indigo and coffeebean weeds that grew among the rice plants. And they mended all the holes made by crawdads on the levee and watched for turtles digging through the mud to push up the roots.

Red-winged blackbirds and rice birds discovered the field. These wild birds had to be shooed away like chickens in a garden. Snipes swooped down, with the wind blowing through their wings like a wild duck's call, to search for insects on the levee. Cranes and white herons fished for the little tow-bellies and shiners that swam in the ditch from the bayou to the field. The ducks and geese came, too, in their autumn flight from the south, and they stayed on longer to eat what they could of the ripening grain.

Jim and Jeff worked together harvesting both rice and cotton crops. It took little time to reap the rice, for the field was a small one and the yield was still not enough to send away to be milled and marketed. But they put it up in sacks to be kept for seed for another year.

"There's enough here to plant all the acres in both our farms," Jim said proudly.

"There's still the question of water," Jeff reminded him. "Still and all," he added when he saw the row of sacks filled with the grain, "Will Fuller ought not to have given up so easy and left the way he did."

The cotton brought no more than in other years, but Jeff and Jim worked together filling the barrels and bottles with Polka Dot Spring Water, and delivering it. And they shared the profits.

"The school at Crossroads is starting up again, and you'll never guess who's coming here to teach it," Kitty said one day as they drove home from church. "It's that little Laura Morse," she went on before anyone had time to answer. "You remember her, Jim."

"Miss Laura!　She was my first teacher

when we still lived in Drew County," Jim exclaimed.

Laura Morse had been their neighbor in Drew County when their parents were alive. She had roamed the pastures and picked blackberries with them all one summer—barefooted and sunbonneted like the rest. Then, suddenly, in the fall she had put up her hair and, dressed in a long skirt and stiff-starched shirtwaist, had got a job teaching the one-room school.

Reuben used to laugh and say you couldn't tell the teacher from the kids in school except that she sat up front at the big desk. And it was true that some of the boys in class were as old as she was, though Jim had just entered the primer class.

"Now you draw an apple on your slate like this, and you draw a little tail here at the side. See! That's the way you write *a*." Jim remembered the way she sat down on the bench beside him, speaking in her soft voice as she gave him his first lesson in writing. "And for an *o* you make a round ring, just the kind your lips make when you say 'Oh.'"

"It's too bad I'm through with school," he said. "Wouldn't she be surprised to see me in the class!"

"Jim Luckett, what do you mean you're through with school? The way you talk, a person would think you knew just about everything there is to know. Of course, you're not through. Reuben and I can carry on your work for you, and you can ride your little old Trinket in to DeVall's Bluff every day and go to the high school."

Jim caught Jeff's eye and saw him nod approval.

"She's right, Jim," Jeff said. "She hadn't talked over any of those plans with me, but I think it's a good idea just the same."

"That's what I'd like to do, but there's one thing troubling me," Jim said hesitatingly. "Now that the war's over, Reuben might be writing any time and saying he wants to sell the farm. And I'd like to have enough money saved up this time to pay him for his share."

"We'll get it up somehow," Jeff insisted. "You'd best go on with your education while you can. There's no telling how long it will be before we hear from Reuben. He might even come back here before he goes off to wherever he aims to settle."

Reuben did return home. There were no parades for him then, as there had been when he went off to war. He came in quietly one

day soon after the harvest was over, again on
a horse he had rented from a livery stable at
DeVall's Bluff.

"I've come back to rest for a while, for I'm
tired, very tired," he said. "Later on, we can
talk about selling the farm and going away
together."

Kitty hovered over him as if he were a child.
She cooked the things he liked best. She
insisted that he take the most comfortable
chair in the room.

But one Sunday afternoon, when they sat
before a warm fire, she said to him, "Reuben,
I want you to take the buggy and go after the
new schoolteacher. It's our time to board her
now. She's stayed at nearly all the other
places on the prairie."

Jim offered to go in Reuben's place, but
Kitty would have none of it. She smiled to
herself as if she had a secret she would not
share. And later on when she looked out the
window and saw Reuben driving up with
Laura Morse, she nodded her head wisely.

"He's not looking so tired now," she said.
"Look at the way he's walking up the path
carrying both her valises in one hand with as
spry a step as he's ever had before.

The young schoolteacher was just as Jim

remembered her to be, with light hair pinned up in little puffs on the top of her head, and eyes the color of blue cornflowers. Her voice was soft, and there was something a little shy about her when she smiled. Reuben's eyes seldom left her, and when he spoke, it was to her that he turned.

"I just can't get over how you've grown up," he kept saying. "Why you were just a child when we lived in Drew County."

"A girl of fifteen seems like a child to a boy when he's nineteen years old," Miss Laura began, then she stopped suddenly and blushed.

"But when he's twenty-seven, four years' difference in age is just about right," Reuben said with a laugh, which made her blush even more than ever.

Reuben spoke little about the fighting he had done. Instead, when anyone asked questions about the war, he told about the coconut palms and the blue Pacific. He talked about bamboo thickets and birds the color of which he had never seen before in all his life.

"They grow rice out in the Philippines," he said. "They call their little patches 'rice paddies.'"

Jim wanted to know more, and Reuben told of how the seeds were sown, first, in beds of rich muddy earth of the faraway tropic islands.

"The men work the soil with their bare toes to keep it soft," he said.   "And when the rice has grown to a fair size, the women take it out to a field flooded over with water and plant each stalk, one by one."

"One stalk at a time!" Jim exclaimed. "How do they find time enough in a day?"

"It's hard work all right," Reuben replied, "but a whole family will work together, husband and wife and all the children big enough to walk. Rice is their bread and meat as well, and they eat it three times a day."

He told of seeing them winnow the rice after the harvest, tossing big baskets of it up to let the wind blow through and carry away the chaff.

"It was a pretty sight, and somehow that part didn't seem like work, the way they laughed and sang while they did it. I used to get a little homesick watching them, all being together and having fun the way they did."

"How big are the farms?" Jim asked.

"Not big. But no matter how little land a fellow has nor how hard he has to work it, it's not bad when he feels it's his own and no overlord has a claim to it or him. That's why they rebelled against the Spaniards and fought them."

"I'd not want an overlord off in some other country laying claim to our place," Jim said. "I'd fight, too, just the way they did."

"Yes, a fellow feels that way," Reuben agreed. "Our grandfathers fought at King's Mountain because they didn't want a foreign government telling them how to run their affairs. That's why I can't help wishing we hadn't taken over the Philippines ourselves. But it's done now, and I hope we keep the promise we made to give them the freedom that they fought so hard for."

Laura Morse slept in Jim's old room in the loft and Jim and Reuben crossed the bayou for supper every evening. As the time passed, it was later and later at night before Reuben could bring himself to leave the fireside where he sat talking with Kitty and Jeff and the young teacher. And when Laura moved on to stay with another family on the prairie, Reuben borrowed Jeff's buggy and went to visit her there. Kitty said nothing but Jim often caught that little secret smile on her face when she watched Reuben driving off.

Winter passed, and Reuben made no mention of leaving the prairie, though he sometimes talked about the things going on in the world outside. There was a man named Marconi who was working on something he called wireless telegraphy. The old look came back to Reuben's eyes when he read about it, and he seemed again to be searching beyond the horizon.

"Oh, I tell you," he said, "there are big things going on in the world!"

CHAPTER XII

☞ WHEN THE SCHOOL TERM WAS over, Laura Morse went back to her home in Drew County, and there was a restlessness again in Reuben's manner. Jim expected any day to hear him say that it was time now to go away, because there was no future on the prairie.

"It wouldn't surprise me a bit if he does," Kitty said. "I've noticed sometimes how he looks off in the distance, as if he were seeing himself somewhere far away."

But Reuben made no mention of leaving, or even of selling the farm. He had added his army pay to the money he had given Jim to keep for him, and he left it untouched in the bank.

The high school term at DeVall's Bluff came to an end, too, and Jim was able to take on his share of the spring planting. Reuben worked alongside of Jeff and Jim from dawn to twilight getting the cleared acres on both farms ready for the crops. He helped with the delivery of the water barrels, too, and seemed to have no separate plans of his own.

Often Reuben and Jim went on trips that lasted several days, going farther and farther afield to sell the Polka Dot Prairie Spring Water.

"If I didn't see the morning sun to the left of me, I'd say for sure we were turned around and heading home again, Jim said one day as they were riding in the wagon beyond the state line, in Louisiana.

They had kept to the low country where there were few springs and where creeks and bayous were sluggish, with water that was scarcely fit to drink. Tiger trotted beside the wagon, and sometimes he jumped up in it to ride, too, then jumped out again when he saw something on the trail he must explore.

They had gone through forests of melancholy cypresses, and out on the open plain, camping each night beside the road, and cooking game they had hunted along the way, over an open fire.

Now, after many days, they found themselves on a prairie with the same wide-circled horizon as their own. And the same line of trees, like shaggy eyebrows, bordered a bayou in the distance.

The few houses they passed were no more than unpainted shacks, with sagging stoops and mudpacked chimneys. There were a few flowers growing in front of the doorways but little farming. Quite clearly these were the homes of people who lived off the wild land by hunting and fishing.

Reuben and Jim were all the more surprised when they came to a neat white farmhouse, surrounded by fields of rice growing green and lush above the water. A man with a fishing pole across his shoulder called out a greeting to them as he passed along the road walking toward the bayou. But he spoke in a language Jim had never heard before.

"He was talking French," Reuben explained when the man had gone on his way. "I knew a Frenchman up in Alaska, and that's the way he talked. This must be where the French came after they were driven out of Canada by the British. The Cajuns. You read about it in Longfellow's poem, Evangeline."

"It must be the part of the country where William Fuller saw rice growing for the first time, too," Jim said. "He talked about fields of it like these, only when he came through it was the fall of the year and it was ripe and headed, and ready for harvesting."

Reuben did not answer, for his mind was still on the poem, and he recited a few lines haltingly, searching back in his memory for the words.

> Beautiful is the land, with its prairies
> and forests of fruit trees;
> Under the feet a garden of flowers,
> and the bluest of heavens
> Bending above, and resting its dome
> on the walls of the forest.
> They who dwell there have named it
> the Eden of Louisiana

"How did you know that poetry?" Jim asked. "Did you learn the lines the year you went to high school in Drew County? We had that poem in school this year but I sure couldn't recite it now!"

Reuben's face turned red.

"Miss Laura read the whole poem to me

one evening, and I had her go over that part till I could say it by heart. Somehow it put me in mind of our own prairie in the spring-time," he said.

Then Reuben did love the prairie! Jim said to himself. Loved it the way he and Jeff and Kitty did!

As if he could read Jim's thought, Reuben began to argue out loud. "The prairie gets a hold on you," he muttered, "but yet there's the world outside where things are happening. A man can make a fortune in electricity or wireless telegraph if he just picked the right thing.

"And how can you get ahead," he went on, "get married, maybe, and raise a family if you can't even raise a crop that will bring some money in?"

Without answering, Jim turned the wagon into the farmyard gate and drew up at the door of the house to leave a sample of drinking water.

The whole family clustered about the kitchen door and invited the strangers in. The farmer's wife was Acadian (Cajun her husband called it). She spoke to the children in her own language but to her husband in English.

The farmer was a Northerner. From Idaho, he explained. His father had fought in the Union Army in the Civil War and had talked all his life about the pretty country he'd marched across as a soldier.

"So, when I grew up I came to see for myself," the man added. "And I stayed."

He tasted the Polka Dot Prairie Water, drinking it from a gourd. "It's good," he said. "But we've got a good well. All the folks around here have good well water. It's farther down around the bayou where they need drinking water."

Jim nodded. "I thought that would be so. This is like the part of Arkansas where we come from. The real reason I stopped was to see how you grow your rice."

"It's a funny thing," the Yankee farmer answered. "Another fellow came by here once asking the same thing. He and the fellow he was traveling with stayed at Abbott's farm half a day just looking at the rice and the well and the pump rigging. But I don't know where he was from."

Jim thought he knew who that other man had been. He could almost see William Fuller like a shadow behind them as they trudged out to the fields. They walked gingerly along the edge of the flooded terraces toward the chugging pumps.

"Rice is a pretty thing," the farmer said proudly. "But you sure have to know how to grow it. They tell me down at Dusen's—down the road apiece—there's a hired man working just to learn how rice is grown. Seems like everybody and his brother has suddenly taken a notion to try out rice."

"Not everybody," Reuben laughed. "Just folks that can't raise a regular crop on hard-baked blue clay soil near a bayou."

Instead of turning back when they left the farm, Jim wanted to drive on to the bayou.

"This is too far to come to sell our water," Reuben objected. "No matter how much they need it."

"I know. But I'm thinking about Mr. Fuller. It must have been William Fuller and Hewitt Puryear who stopped at that farm the time they were on a hunting trip and brought back my seed. But who is the hired man working only to learn how rice is grown?"

"What's it to you, who he is?" Reuben teased.

Jim didn't answer but he pulled the reins to keep Trinket at an even slower pace than usual. They found the Dusen farm, as Jim thought they would, by reading the names on mailboxes.

Jim pulled Trinket to a stop. He could see a man coming across the field from the barn with a cricket of eggs in his hand. The man was in faded blue jeans with a straw hat on his head and he looked as you would expect a hired man to look.

But he didn't bear any resemblance to William Fuller. Jim sighed and was about to drive on when the man waved his battered wide-brimmed hat and spoke politely urging the travelers to come in and stay awhile. That's just the way people acted on Polka Dot Prairie. It was a treat to folks in lonesome places to see a stranger and it wouldn't be kind to disappoint the man by refusing to stop.

"Howdy," the man said. "Just go in and make yourselves at home. Mrs. Dusen'll be happy to welcome you."

Jim and Reuben tied Trinket under a shade tree and walked up the path to the house. Mrs. Dusen was in the kitchen when they knocked but she wiped her hands on her apron and led them to the parlor.

"Your hired man told us to come on in," Reuben began. But he got no further, for just then the man in the faded blue jeans walked into the parlor and sat down.

"It won't be long now till we'll be having dinner," he said. "You'd best stay on and join us. It's mighty pleasant to have company at table, ain't it, Ma?"

Mrs. Dusen smiled and nodded.

Waiting for the hired man, Mrs. Dusen had said! Then this must be the owner of the farm, himself. Jim was covered with confusion but Reuben seemed not to mind the mistake at all.

Two small, barefoot children had been staring shyly through the parlor door. Reuben grinned at them and they came up to him willingly. Soon he was telling them stories about Alaska and California and the Philippines, talking more freely than Jim had ever heard him about the places he'd been.

"Yonder he comes," Mrs. Dusen said, looking out of the window. Now we can eat."

She bustled out to the kitchen and Jim looked up to see a short, heavy-set man with a goatee coming into the room.

"Mr. Fuller!" he exclaimed.

"Why, hello, young fellow," William Fuller came forward with a pleased smile. "I didn't expect to find you here so far from home."

"And I didn't expect to find you here either," Jim answered. "I thought maybe you'd gone to a city, looking—like Reuben used to—for big things in the world."

"So I am," William Fuller answered, "looking for something big—but not in a city. Are you moving away from Prairie County?" Mr. Fuller asked, as he shook hands with Reuben.

"No, we're not," Jim answered quickly. "But there are not many left there now."

"Yes, I know," Fuller said, and a troubled expression crossed his face.

"Even you—"

"Even I?" Fuller said in surprise. "Do you mean the people there think I've left the prairie without any intention of coming back?"

Jim had to admit it was true.

"No," William Fuller said. "Those who know me better know that's not true. I decided to come down here and work on a rice farm to learn all there is to know about raising rice. I must find out what mistakes I made when I tried it myself, so I'll know how to succeed when I plant again on my own farm."

"And I'm here to say there's nothing he's not finding out about," Mr. Dusen spoke up. "He's in the fields, at the pumps, and working with the binder and thresher. Sometimes I think he'd like to take them all apart and put them back together again just to see what makes them work."

After they had eaten dinner, Mr. Fuller took Jim and Reuben over the place to show them how the fields had been leveled and how the water was pumped on. And he told them about how the grains would be threshed and harvested later on. He listened carefully when Jim told about the patch of rice he had raised.

"Some others have tried it too," Fuller said. "I've kept up with a few folks at Hazen and I'm told that the Morris brothers and Jack Noble in the timber country have been growing a little. But their patches are small like your own and watered from the bayous the way yours is.

"I'm sure our prairie is good rice land, but I'm staying on here until I've mastered every step in growing rice on a large scale. Then you'll see me back at my own farm."

"How long will it be, Mr. Fuller?" Reuben interrupted. "How long before we'll know whether our land's fit for use or not?"

"Impatient, are you?" William Fuller said. "That's because you're young. And yet, being

young, you can spare a year from your life better than I can."

The afternoon shadows were long before they had seen all there was to see and turned Trinket up the road for the long trip home. The two brothers were silent, Reuben's eyes restless and on far horizons.

Jim tried to follow his brother's thoughts. "He's thinking about Miss Laura Morse," he said to himself. "Thinking he wants to marry her, I bet. But he won't do it till he's making a living. The prairie or the outside world? There's just no telling how Reuben is going to choose."

They slept under the wagon that night and before they quite fell asleep, Jim asked Reuben to say the lines from Evangeline again.

"I guess Miss Laura must be a pretty good teacher," Jim said, "to have taught you all that poetry."

CHAPTER XIII

◑ IT WAS TWO YEARS LATER THAT William Fuller returned to his home. He brought seed rice and machinery with him, and he worked all winter, putting in his well. Two mustang ponies walked around in circles to turn the pulley that brought up bucket after bucket of dirt, and neighbors helped with the digging. They struck water at thirty feet, and still they drilled, deeper and deeper until at last they reached a hundred and fifty feet down in the earth. The pump was set in a pit walled up with boards.

On the prairie it seemed as if time had stood

still. A little more rain one season; a little less, the next. A few more families moving away; a few—a very few—moving in. But there was the same gloom at cotton ginning time; the same hopes for improvements put aside.

Jim had finished the three-year course at the high school and Kitty was trying to talk him into going to college. She tried to talk to Reuben, too, about his future, but her words fell on deaf ears.

Both Reuben and Jim worked their land as best they could; they helped Jeff and sold barrels of water wherever they could. But they both seemed to be waiting for something —waiting, waiting.

Then a man drove by the farm one morning and said that William Fuller had come home.

Hope returned to the prairie! Men made excuses to ride out each day to look on at the work that was done at Fuller's farm. They no longer joked and laughed and said it couldn't be done. Instead there were some who met at Crossroads post office and collected money among themselves until they had a thousand dollars. They put this sum in a bank as a prize for William Fuller.

"It's yours if you can prove rice can be

raised on this prairie land," the men said.
"But you'll have to produce a crop of at least
thirty-five bushels to the acre to prove it."

People came from all over the county, and
from nearby counties to help level the field of
seventy acres Mr. Fuller had plowed. Finally
it was as smooth as a parlor floor. Then
levees of dirt were thrown up four to eight
inches high on every two-inch slope of land.

William Fuller was taking no chances now.
He seemed to be everywhere on the field, doing
much of the work himself, and stopping to
explain carefully to all who were there to help
him.

Every time they went out selling spring
water, Reuben and Jim would manage to guide
the horse in the direction of Hazen.

Reuben still read about great things being
done in the cities of the North but he made
no mention of wanting to go. The rice fields
at William Fuller's farm held him.

The rice came up, a fresh, young green
stretching far out toward the horizon, seventy
acres of it. The wind blew softly through it,
making a rippling movement as if hundreds
of kittens were playing underneath an immense carpet.

When the rice had grown four inches high,

the water was turned on and the whole field was flooded. Four hundred gallons to the minute came tumbling through the ditches and onto the fields. And the hard, blue clay beneath the top soil held the water and would not let it sink deep to disappear underground.

The rice grew five feet tall, and turned to a tawny ripe color, with the heavy heads of grain drooping gracefully. The neighboring farmers left their own poor crops again to help, this time with the harvesting. They worked together, with sickles swinging. Never before had the prairie yielded such a bountiful harvest. They made guesses about the number of bushels there would be in all.

"Now I'm a good enough hand to guess a cotton crop, but this is something I wouldn't even try to judge," one old man said to another. "But in all my days I've never seen a healthier crop of anything on this prairie."

The rice was left to dry in shocks out in the field. Seventy acres of mounds, like squat, hooded men that alone knew the secret of whether the prize would be won or lost.

"Just suppose there are thirty-four instead of thirty-five bushels to the acre," Kitty said with a worried air. "What will happen then?"

"As far as I can make out, Mr. Fuller'll get nothing unless the yield is thirty-five for every acre," Jeff replied.

On the day of the threshing and weighing, the road leading to the Fuller farm was crowded with every kind of wagon, and surreys, buggies and carriages as well. There was even a horseless carriage there, chugging down the road and frightening the horses so that everyone had to get out and hold the reins as it went by.

More than a thousand people were there on that day. They came from every county in Arkansas. Jeff's parents had come all the way from Little Rock. Laura Morse came, too, surprising everyone but Reuben, who seemed to have known about it all along.

Lunches were spread out on the ground, or eaten in wagons, and no one made a move to go home until the rice was measured and the bushels counted.

"William Fuller has won!" The cry went up and was repeated like a wave on the wind. Five thousand, two hundred and twenty-five bushels from a seventy-acre tract!

Jim did some quick figuring and clutched Jeff's arm. "That's more than seventy-five bushels to the acre!" he shouted. "He's more than doubled his goal!   Hurrah for Fuller!"

A feeling of exultation spread through the crowd.   Strangers talked to each other as if they had been close friends all their lives. They made plans as they went back to their homes, of how they, too, would put in wells and terrace their own land with levees to hold the water for the rice they would grow.   Rice would save the Prairie!

Reuben and Laura Morse rode back in the buggy, and Kitty and Jeff with his parents went in the wagon with Jim.   They passed the vacant farmhouses along the way and they knew that soon smoke would be rising from the chimneys.   The fields would be green

again, with rice growing tall and heavy with grain.

"I figure there'll be people moving into the towns, too, filling up those vacant stores," Jeff remarked. "There'll be machine shops needed. And well companies, and carpenters will be kept mighty busy, too, with new buildings that will be going up."

"And there'll be a rice mill," Jim said.

They were still talking of the days to come when they arrived at the Brooks' farm to find Reuben and Laura waiting there for them.

"When we build the parlor, I want to add two more bedrooms as well," Kitty said as they sat down to supper. "One will be for Lucy, so she can have a room to herself, and one will be a spare room for company that comes visiting."

"We're going to have to go a little slow at first," Jeff warned. "It'll take a lot of money to buy well-rigging enough to flood a big farm."

"It would be better, I think if we could work together on it," Jim ventured. "We could put in the rigging here the first year. Then with the money the first rice crop brings, we could fix up our place across the bayou."

"You've been saving up to pay me for my

share in the place, haven't you, Jim?" Reuben asked.

"Yes," Jim answered, waiting to hear what else Reuben would say.

Would he go off now, in search of new horizons? To hunt for gold or to make horseless carriages? All the others looked up, too, their eyes on Reuben.

"Well, you can put up that money toward the well, for I've decided we'll all keep the farm together the way we'd planned when we first bought it. And I've that money in the bank that can be added to yours and Jeff's. That ought to be enough."

Kitty laughed, happily. "I vow, Reuben. You had me wondering for a minute. I thought for sure you were going to say you'd be on your way somewhere in a day or so."

"Well, I've been thinking, there are big things happening in the world outside. But there are big things going on right here in our own home," Reuben said. "And there's something else," he added with a glance toward Laura, "we might add a few rooms to our own house, too, for it'll be a little crowded for three people to live in."